MW01096399

Walker's American History
series for young people

Message
from the
Mountains

Message
from the
Mountains

Edith McCall

Walker and Company
New York

Walker's American History Series for Young People
Series Editor, Frances Nankin

First published in the United States of America by the Walker Publishing Company, Inc.

Published simultaneously in Canada by John Wiley & Sons Canada, Limited, Rexdale, Ontario.

Library of Congress Cataloging in Publication Data

McCall, Edith S.
    Message from the mountains.
    (Walker's American history series for young people)
    Summary: In the frontier town of Franklin, Missouri, in 1826, teenage friends Jim Mathews and Kit Carson share the dream of running away to a life of adventure on the Santa Fe Trail.
    1. Children's stories, American. [1. Carson, Kit, 1809-1868—Fiction. 2. Missouri—Fiction. 3. West (U.S.)—Fiction] I. Title. II. Series.
PZ7.M1229Mes   1985   [Fic]   85-3142
ISBN 0-8027-6582-3

Book Design by Teresa M. Carboni

Printed in the United States of America

10 9 8 7 6 5 4 3 2 1

ACKNOWLEDGMENTS

Many sources were consulted for the factual background of this fictional tale. Old files of *The Missouri Intelligencer* and *Boon's Lick Advertiser*, published in Franklin, Missouri, from 1819 through 1826, acquainted me with leading citizens of the town and events of those early years. A person in the offices of Howard County, Missouri, helped me reconstruct the basic layout of old Franklin; to have imagined the original town without that help would have been most difficult, as early Franklin was washed away long ago by the Missouri River.

Among the books from which I drew my information, of special importance are Henry Inman's *The Old Santa Fe Trail*, H. E. Stocking's *The Road to Santa Fe*, and *Missouri: A Guide to the "Show Me" State*, compiled by the Works Progress Administration Writers' Program. From the latter, I learned of the racetrack in Franklin and the "goose pull" event.

Most of all, I am indebted to M. Morgan Estergreen, who, in *Kit Carson: A Portrait in Courage*, provided the information that Kit Carson borrowed a mule on which to ride to the West. It was that detail which inspired the creation of this story.

Edith McCall
Hollister, Missouri
1985

CONTENTS

A NOTE FROM THE AUTHOR

This story takes place in 1826, before the first wagon trains of pioneer settlers went west and before the Rocky Mountain and Pacific coastal lands became part of the United States. The Missouri and Mississippi Rivers formed the western boundaries to the Louisiana Purchase, land bought from France in 1803. Missouri was the westernmost state and Missouri's outermost settlement large enough to be called a town was Franklin, about halfway across the state on the north bank of the Missouri River. With the exception of a few ferry crossings, one trading post and Fort Osage, there was not a single town west of Franklin for nine hundred miles until one reached the Mexican village called Santa Fe, which is now in the state of New Mexico.

In 1826, Franklin, Missouri, was a busy place. It was there that the famous Santa Fe Trail started, where wagons and pack animals were loaded with cloth, hardware, tobacco, and whatever else a trader could get and believed he could sell or trade in the old Mexican town. Steamboats from the South and East docked at the riverfront to unload goods for Franklin merchants to sell in their stores. Near the river were warehouses for storing shipments, and there were factories where workers made rope and cigars from the hemp and tobacco grown by farmers nearby. Inns bustled with people who arrived by wagon or on horseback from St. Louis, preparing to go with the next caravan. Others had just returned from Santa Fe.

It was always a busy time when a caravan returned. The men brought back herds of Mexican mules or the donkeys used to breed them. Raising mules was a new business in Missouri. Mules were in demand as sturdy animals, valuable for traveling on the Trail and for farm work. The travelers also brought back Mexican gold and silver, along with tales of their adventures in the little-known western lands.

Young people who lived in Franklin saw the gold and silver and heard the tales. Many dreamed of heading west with a Santa Fe caravan, their imaginations stirred by thoughts of riches, unknown lands, and the adventures of those who stayed in the mountains to become fur trappers and hunters. One of the Franklin boys who longed to go west was Kit Carson, who went on to become a famous scout and fur trader. Kit's parents were pioneer settlers who farmed on the frontier lands. History books tell us that when Kit was sixteen, in September 1826, he ran away from Franklin and the saddle shop where he was an apprentice. We also know that three of Kit's brothers were with the caravan he joined, as well as Charles and William Bent, fur traders who later became famous for building an important trading post. This trading post, built on the banks of the Arkansas River, was called Bent's Fort. Kit Carson, his older brothers and half brothers, and the Bents are all characters in this story. Other people named in this story are also real people, such as George Caleb Bingham, who later became a famous artist.

We know something else about the boy Kit Carson. He borrowed a mule from someone in Franklin on the night he ran away. Riding this mule, he caught up with the caravan and was hired by Charles Bent to "ride cavvy." This meant he was to keep the loose animals moving along with the rest of the group. Kit is said to have started the borrowed mule on its way back to Franklin as soon as he was able to. He went all the way to Santa Fe, and from there into the mountains north of the Mexican town, beginning his life as a fur trapper.

Who would lend Kit a mule to help him start his life's adventure? I wondered about that, and this story is built on a possible answer to that question. It seemed to me that it must have been someone who could understand and even share Kit's wish to go west, someone who also dreamed of a life of adventure and excitement. I thought it might have been someone about his own age, perhaps a close friend he saw often while he was apprenticed to the saddlemakers in Franklin. This is the story of that friend, a boy I've named Jim Mathews. It could have happened like this. . . .

Message
from the
Mountains

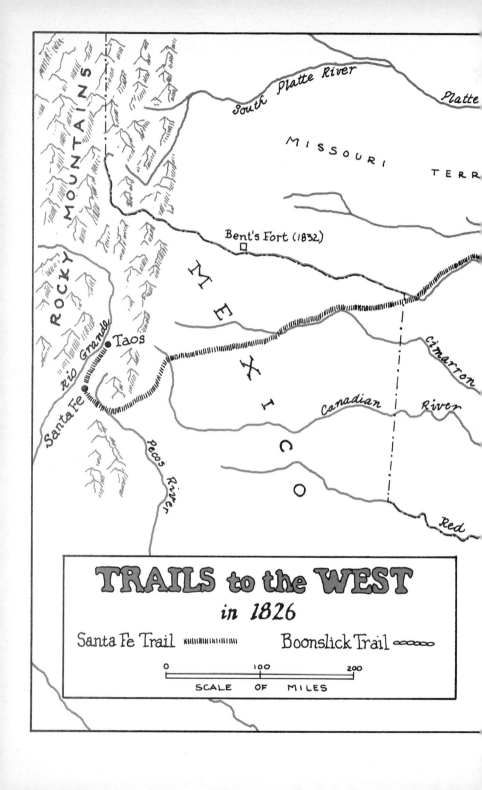

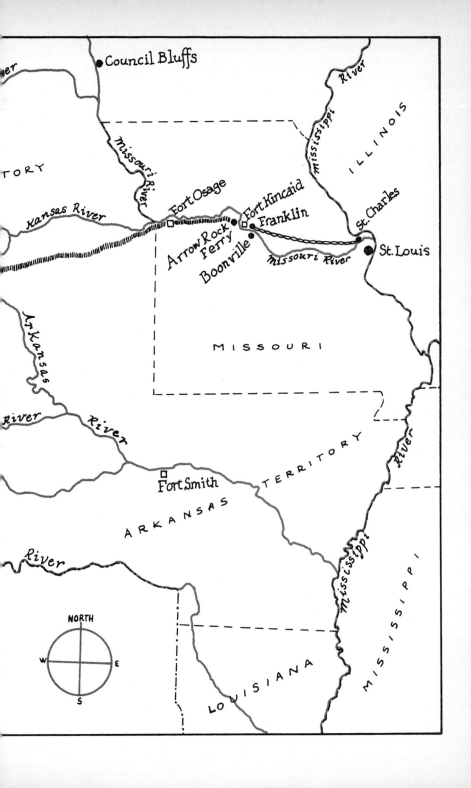

1
Return of the Caravan

JIM Mathews was the first in Mr. Hood's store to hear the distant shouts that August afternoon in 1826. They came faintly from the west but were loud enough to be heard in the frontier town of Franklin, Missouri.

Jim, who had been sweeping out the dust from a dark corner behind the vinegar barrel, stopped his work and stood motionless. His slim body was tense, his brown eyes bright with hope. He straightened up, pushed back his dark hair, and listened to be sure he had really heard the sounds for which he had been waiting so long.

"Yahoo! Haw, there! Ya-*hoo-oo*!"

Then, from far off, but distinctly, came the sharp rapid static of riflefire.

It had to be. There was no mistaking those sounds. They were the joyful salute of men returning to Franklin after the long journey to Santa Fe, in Mexico. It just had to be Pa's caravan—the one that had left Franklin four months ago. Pa would be back at last!

The boy leaned his broom against a counter and fumbled to undo the tie-strings of his apron. Self-conscious, he felt a twinge of embarrassment about his clothes. His homespun brown trousers were now so short that four

1

inches of thin tanned leg showed above each ankle and bare foot. Luckily, the strings of his shiny black apron didn't go into a knot. He slipped the neck strap over his head and tossed the apron onto the counter.

"Good-bye, old broom," Jim said softly. "I may never be using you again!" He started for the front of the store thinking about Pa's promise that when he returned the two of them would become partners. Together they were going fur-trading out west.

He went past the tall tins of tea, the kegs of nails, and the bundles of hemp fiber and bearskins stacked on the rough wooden floorboards. But at the open doorway his conscience stopped him. He looked back at Mr. Hood, who was busily measuring a length of calico cloth for a lady on the other side of the store.

"Mr. Hood, sir, the caravan is back!" he called, and was out the door without waiting for an answer. He couldn't risk waiting, in case his employer stopped him.

With one step and a jump, he was off the wooden walkway along the front of the log building. His feet raised little puffs of dust as he thudded across the unpaved street to the grass of the open public square. He passed the town's well in the center of the square without even seeing Martha Lowry, who was drawing a bucket of water to carry to her home two blocks away.

Jim usually watched for Martha's arrival at the well. When Mr. Hood could spare him, he would go out and lift the heavy bucket for her, unhooking it from the well rope. He would even carry the water home for her if there were no customers in the store and Mr. Hood said it was all right to leave.

"Jim Mathews, whatever is your hurry?" he heard Martha call after him.

"Excuse me, Martha!" He paused just long enough to look back at her. Martha was balancing the water bucket on the edge of the well. Even in his hurry Jim noticed how pretty her red-gold hair looked with the sun shining on it, but her usually sunshiny face looked more as if a storm were brewing.

"Pa's caravan is coming!" he called out. "I've got to go meet him!" He was on his way again, not even seeing Martha set down the heavy bucket and start after him.

"I'll go with you! Wait a minute!"

But Jim didn't hear Martha's call. He was just beyond the market house at the southwestern corner of the square and was starting down the street that headed out of town. Martha stopped, still in the grassy square. Another boy ran toward her, but he, too, ran right by with only a quick wave of the hand. His eyes were on Jim, who was about to disappear from sight.

"Hey, Jim! Wait for me!" the boy yelled as loud as he could.

This time Jim heard the call. He stopped to wait for Kit Carson, his best friend. Kit was apprenticed to the Franklin saddlemakers, William and David Workman. He was seldom allowed to leave the saddlery before suppertime, and Jim was surprised but also pleased to see him now.

As he waited impatiently for Kit, Jim saw Martha looking at him, her hands on her hips. Jim waved, but only to see her turn away with a flip of her long skirt and a toss of the braids that hung down her back almost to her waist.

As soon as Kit caught up to Jim, the two ran on, thudding along the dusty street that headed west for four blocks. There the street became the start of the Santa Fe Trail. The boys had often walked out that way, planning how someday they both would go with a caravan. For five years they had seen men with their caravans of wagons follow the Santa Fe Trail—since 1821, when the first little band took a train of pack mules carrying American goods all the way to Santa Fe. The trail was nearly a thousand miles long, heading first to the west, and then southwest to Mexico. Franklin was the only town in all that distance.

"Hey, Kit! Look!" Jim pointed westward. "See the dust clouds? The caravan's coming for sure!"

Kit was panting. "Yeah—but slow down a little. My legs aren't as long as yours."

"All right, shorty. We can stop for a minute. The caravan's still more'n a mile away, I'd guess."

The two stood at the edge of the road, and Kit pushed back his thick golden-brown hair, dark with dampness at his brow. Kit was older than Jim by more than a year—sixteen last December to Jim's fifteen—but he looked younger. He was short, stocky, and round-faced.

Jim was peering down the road. "Listen," he said. "You can hear the pounding of all those hooves! Sounds like thunder rumbling, doesn't it? Come on, Kit. Let's go!"

The two went on at an easy jog. As they passed the last log house on the edge of Franklin, they reached a gentle slope that ran parallel to the Missouri River through open country.

A dark shape, shrouded in dust, came slowly toward them. To the boys, the shape looked like a dark dragon with a long dusty tail behind it. Only the riders in the lead were in clear view. As they watched, three riders separated from the main body and came toward them.

Jim ran ahead again. "Here come the lead riders!" he called back.

"Wait up!" Kit panted. Jim stopped in the shade of a big maple tree. Both boys' shirts were dark with sweat, and their feet were gray-brown with dust.

"I'm clean tuckered out," Kit said. "Let's sit down on the grass and wait a bit. They'll all get here before long anyway."

A road from the north met the trail near the big tree. All the men would come to that juncture, and some would turn off to herd the animals into a big pasture just outside of Franklin.

"Pa will likely turn off here," Jim said. "He's good with the mules, and I'm guessing he'll be near the end of the caravan, riding herd."

"One of my brothers—William or Ham—might be an advance man," Kit said. "I'm looking for both of them to be with the caravan, and Robert, too."

Now the three lead riders were close, and the boys got to their feet. The men shouted and each raised his arm, pointing a pistol upward. They passed the boys in a roar of gunfire, racing to be the first into Franklin.

"Was one of them your brother?" Jim asked.

Kit shook his head. "No. William and Ham are both taller than those fellas. Couldn't have been Robert, either, and we don't look for Andrew to come back yet." Kit was from a large family with three much older half brothers and two full brothers, who were all in the western fur trade.

The riders had stirred up more dust, and the boys stepped back a bit to avoid breathing it. When it settled, they saw that the main body of the caravan was still about half a mile away.

"Be a while before the next ones get here," Jim said. "Might as well sit down again."

"When I go west, I'm not comin' back," Kit said, leaning back against the tree trunk. "I'm gonna be like my brother Moses. I'll be a trapper and live in the mountains, trapping beaver and not seeing anyone for months." He paused, then added, "Whatever I do, it's not gonna be sitting here in Franklin making saddles or fancy buggy harness for city people. I'm heading west just as soon as I can."

Jim grinned. "I'll be there waiting for you, Kit. Pa said he would take me with him on the next caravan—couple of weeks from now, maybe. He's gonna use the money he gets from this trip to buy some more trading goods, and the two of us are going to Santa Fe together."

"Gee, Jim—I'd sure like to go along. If my pa were still alive, I bet he'd let me go." Kit sighed. His father had been killed in a forest fire. His mother had remarried.

"My stepdaddy says I have to wait another year, till my 'prenticeship is over," he went on. "He says after that I could earn a good livin' as a journeyman saddlemaker and go wherever I please. But I don't want to be a saddlemaker, so why should I wait?"

"Then come along with us when Pa and I go. Get your brothers to say you can. Likely at least one of them'll be going back on the next caravan."

"That would be great. I just might do that." He looked up and nudged Jim. "Look who's comin'—Coy Colton and his two toadies."

A big, husky boy was coming toward them on the road from the flour mill north of Franklin. Coy worked at the mill, and his torn shirt and too-short trousers were so dusty with flour that it was hard to tell what color they really were. Behind him were two younger boys.

"Let's pretend we don't see them," Jim said. "Every time I talk to that guy he makes me mad."

Jim and Kit stood up and turned away, keeping their eyes on the road to the west. The main body of the caravan was much nearer now.

Coy and his friends walked faster and stepped in front of Jim and Kit, blocking their view.

"Well, look who's here," Coy said to Jim. "Daddy's skinny beanpole, out to meet him. And the little saddlemaker, too," he said to Kit. "We'll wait here in the shade with you nice little boys."

Jim could feel his body tense. He pressed his lips together to keep from speaking.

Kit put a hand on his friend's arm. "Easy," he said in a low voice. Then, louder, he added, "Come on, Jim. Let's go meet the caravan."

The first wagon, with men riding horseback on both sides of it, was now a short distance away. The riders couldn't resist speeding up as they neared the town, and their shouting, shooting, and dust filled the air as they galloped past. The long line of creaking wagons came on slowly, and behind them was a herd of mules and horses with the riders who tended them.

Jim started to walk away with Kit, edging around Coy. "No, we don't want you nice boys to go yet," Coy said. He thrust out a dirty foot and hooked it around Jim's ankle. Jim fell on the grass, but he jumped quickly back on his feet. He was ready to strike out at Coy until he felt an insistent tug from Kit.

"Come on, Jim."

Kit's grip was firm, and Jim, thinking more clearly, moved away before Coy could stop him. Coy didn't try to follow.

"That guy is so big he could beat both of us to a pulp," Kit said. "And you know he uses those two smaller kids to hold you down. You wouldn't stand a chance, Jim."

Leaving the shady place to Coy and his friends, Jim and Kit watched eagerly for familiar faces on drivers and riders. The noise was too loud for talk now over the shouting, the creaking of wagon wheels, and the thud of hooves. Jim looked for his father among the mule handlers, knowing he was an expert at handling stock. A large part of the trading goods from Franklin—cloth, guns, kettles and other hardware—was sold in Santa Fe for Spanish gold or silver, but some of the goods went for Mexican mules, horses, and donkeys. Missouri farmers and traders—even farmers from east of the Mississippi—valued those sturdy mules. All the ones brought back were quickly sold.

Kit shouted into Jim's ear, "I think I see my brother Robert! See you later!" He ran after one of the passing wagons near the end of the line.

The men riding herd approached, and as the herd reached the junction, they turned the animals toward the big pasture where they would be sold. Buyers would come from St. Louis, St. Charles, and even from the lead-mining regions of southeastern Missouri, eager to have their pick of the animals.

Jim watched anxiously for a glimpse of his father. The dust was so thick that the herders had pulled kerchiefs over their noses and mouths, and it was hard to recognize faces. He was soon coughing from the dust, and his eyes were smarting. Then his heart jumped. Coming toward him was a tall, slender rider on a mule.

Jim ran to meet him. "Pa! Here I am! It's me, Pa—"

The man glanced Jim's way and rode his mule past him to the street leading to the town square. Jim stopped. He had been mistaken. He should have known that wasn't his pa. Pa rode with his shoulders squared, and this man was slouched over. Turning again, he watched the last of the herders as they moved the animals toward the pasture lot.

Then there were no more animals or riders on the trail. He waited, but his father was not among the men who came back from the pasture. The last of them barred the gates and passed Jim, heading for town after the long journey across mountains and plains.

How did I miss him? Jim wondered. *He must have been on the other side of the wagons or the herd. Maybe he's in town already, looking for me while I stand out here!*

Everyone had gone back into town, even Coy and his buddies. Jim began to run. He reached the square just as the last of the wagon teams was being unhitched on the open grassy area. The usually quiet town was bedlam now. Harnesses jangled. Men shouted, "Whoa, there! Back, back—come on now, move along!" Horses whinnied and stomped the ground, and mules brayed. Above it all rose the sound of laughter and shouting from men free at last from the drudgery of the long overland journey. The celebration of their return was already well underway.

Jim's eyes searched the crowd. Long bars of sunlight cut through the dust, turning the gray particles to gold and making happy weathered faces glow. The boy looked for that special face, lean and brown and surely also searching for a glimpse of his son. He joined the crowd on the walk opposite the street where Mr. Hood's store was and passed the new, two-story log jail. Two whiskered faces were pressed against the iron bars of the small windows—no doubt these inmates would have plenty of company as the night wore on.

At McNee's new tavern, a crowd of men stood on the porch. Jim's father, Jed Mathews, was not among them. Then, thinking his pa might be looking for him at Mr. Hood's store, Jim headed across the grassy square, threading his way past the wagons. A familiar figure stood near the well. It was not his pa, but his pa's best friend, Jeremiah Jones. Jim ran toward him.

"Hey, Jeremiah!" The man did not turn.

When he was closer, Jim called again. It was not until he reached out and touched the man's shoulder that the fellow turned. He was taking a great gulp of water from a gourd that hung from the well frame, and he wiped his dripping mustache with his sleeve as he turned.

Jim stared. It was not Jeremiah. He had been wrong again.

"Oh, I thought you were Jeremiah Jones," he said apologetically.

The man put the gourd back on its hook. He drew his hand over his grizzly cheeks before he spoke.

"Wal, son, I'm right happy to say that I'm not Jeremiah Jones, 'cause Jeremiah Jones lies back yonder near the Cimarron."

The words hit Jim like a blow to the stomach. He looked away from the man, trying to realize their meaning. Martha's cedar bucket was beside the well, tipped over in a puddle of water. He saw it, felt the coolness of the wet grass on his feet, but his mind was on what the stranger had said. Jeremiah was dead! He was almost too afraid to ask about his father, but he had to know.

He looked up, but the man was gone.

2

Where Is Jed?

It was as if someone had punched him in the stomach. A few minutes earlier he had been hungry, hoping to take his pa to supper at the Hoods' home. Now he had lost all desire to eat or to be with anyone. Where was Pa? Had he been with Jeremiah Jones? Was Pa buried somewhere out there near the Cimarron too, perhaps left for the wolves to eat?

He stood by the well, his whole world falling to bits.

"Hello, Jim."

It was Martha, back to get her water bucket. She had been standing there a minute or so, waiting for Jim to look up and see her, wondering if she should speak to him. He looked so woebegone. She had never seen him look like this—head down, kind of slumped over, just standing there.

"Hello, Jim." She said it again.

This time his head came up just a little. But he didn't look at her. Instead he bent over to pick up her water bucket, dumping out the last of the water.

"Hello, Martha," he said. "I'll fill up your bucket."

Martha said, "Did you see the men come back? How is your father? Where is he now?"

Jim kept his head down, not wanting her to see the tears stinging his eyes. To give himself time to steady his voice, he lowered the bucket, watching intently to see when it hit the water and bringing it up only half full. As he swished the water about to clean the bucket, Martha studied him.

"What's wrong with you, Jim?" she asked at last. "Cat got your tongue? I asked you a simple question. Where is your father?"

"I'll fill this for you, Martha, and help you carry it." Jim's voice was tight. As he hooked the bucket onto the rope and turned the crank to lower it to the water below, he was careful to keep his face turned away. He heard the bucket hit the water, gave it time to refill, and then began rewinding the rope.

"Your father must have been surprised to see how tall you've grown since he left Franklin," Martha said.

Jim unhooked the bucket from the rope. "Come on. I'll carry this home for you. You shouldn't be out here with all these rough men." He started toward the Lowry home, which was on a street that went west from the square.

Martha fell into step beside him.

"Well, tell me what's bothering you," she said. She sounded a bit angry, and if Jim had been able to look at her, he'd have seen it in her blue eyes.

He swallowed hard to get the lump out of his throat before he answered. "Haven't found my father yet."

He was walking as fast as he could without spilling the water. Martha's home, only a block beyond the square, was just about the finest house in town. It was one of the new frame buildings made of boards sawed out at the sawmill instead of logs. Martha's father was an important businessman in Franklin, and he was also a fine doctor. Soon well-diggers would have a private well finished for the Lowry family, and Martha wouldn't have to carry water from the public well.

The young girl hurried to keep up with her friend, her

red-gold braids tossing. "Well, here, let me carry that myself if you don't want to tell me about it. You go and look for him."

Jim shifted the water bucket to his other hand. "It's on my way. I was going to go to the store and see if he's there, but I think I'll go back to the mule lot first. Pa could still be settling the animals for the night. It takes a long time to water them all and see that there's enough feed. I heard someone say they brought back about four hundred to sell. 'Spect Pa's been right busy. So I'll go back out there."

I've got to ask some of the men if Jeremiah was alone at the Cimarron River, he told himself.

"What if he isn't there?" Martha asked.

"Someone will know where he is, or there'll be a message from him telling me he waited for the next caravan. He wouldn't just stay out in those mountains and not send a message to let me know what's happening."

Martha took hold of his free arm.

"So that's it. You don't know what's happened at all. Why didn't you tell me right away?"

Jim felt the lump coming back. *I can't cry, not in front of her,* he thought. He didn't answer her question.

She let go of his arm, giving it just the tiniest squeeze. "You're right, Jim. He's sent a message. He's such a nice man and he knows you've been counting on his getting back so's the two of you can get ready to go trapping. But more'n likely, you'll find him around somewhere."

They had reached the Lowry house. Jim carried the bucket into the kitchen and set it on a big pine table.

Old Emily, the Lowrys' servant, was peeling potatoes. She had worked for the Lowry family since before Martha was born, before they came to Franklin from Kentucky, and had helped watch over Martha all the girl's life.

" 'Bout time you got here with that water, Martha," she scolded. "Young ladies ain't s'posed to be out starin' at them trader men. If your ma knew what you were up to, she'd be in here scoldin' you right now. Now get me a dipper of that water for these potatoes. Folks has got to eat, even on the day them shoutin' traders gets back to town."

She glanced at Jim who was waiting by the door to say good-bye. "I plumb forgot your daddy was one of them traders now, Jim. How did he make the trip?"

Jim had stepped out of the warm kitchen. "I gotta go, Emily. Martha will tell you about my pa." Then he ran around the corner of the house and headed for the street. He went westward a block or two and then south to the street he and Kit had followed.

As he drew near the big corral, he heard the noises of the animals, but he could scarcely see any of them for the dust. A few men were filling tanks with buckets of water from the new well at a corner of the feedlot.

At the fence, he studied the dim figures of the men, seeking a certain tall, slender form. Most of them wore kerchiefs over their mouths and noses, their faces hidden further under broad-brimmed hats. It was hard to recognize anyone. Off to the left, Jim saw a tall figure leaving the lot on foot.

His heart leaped. Those long, sure steps brought memories of Pa striding homeward from a day's work in the fields, memories of the farm where they had lived until his mother died about two years ago.

"Pa! Wait for me!" Jim shouted. The man didn't turn. But it was hard to shout loud enough to be heard over all the noise. *He didn't hear me,* Jim thought, and ran after the long-legged man.

"Pa! Wait! It's me—Jim!"

He had almost reached him when the man heard his call. Looking back for just a moment, the man paused and took off his broad-brimmed hat. The long rays of the sun cast a glow on his thick red hair. He pulled down his kerchief, uncovering a shaggy red beard. Without speaking, he turned and went on.

Another mistake! Jim wondered how he could have been so wrong again. This man didn't look anything like his pa. Pa might have grown a beard while he was gone, but his hair was dark brown, like Jim's. Then Jim had an idea. Perhaps this man knew Jed Mathews. He ran to catch up with the stranger, who was about to turn into the street that led to the square. The man didn't seem inclined to stop and talk, so Jim tried to match his stride.

"Mister," he said, "do you know my father, Jed Mathews?"

The man slowed his long steps for just a moment, turning to look at Jim. The boy saw impatience in his face, but there was also a softening of the bright blue eyes.

"Jed Mathews? Yeah—I knew him. You his boy? He was always talking about a boy back in Franklin."

"Folks say I look a lot like him, now that I'm growing tall," Jim said eagerly. "Is he still back there in the horse and mule lot?"

"No," the man said. "He ain't there." His step lengthened again, and Jim walked faster too.

"You saw him, then?"

"Not since we left Santa Fe."

They were halfway to the square now, and the voices of the celebrators could be heard. Jim waited for the man to tell him more, but he strode on in silence.

He touched the man's sleeve. "You mean he didn't start out with the caravan?"

"That's right, boy."

Jim's disappointment was mixed with a feeling of relief. At least his father had not died near the Cimarron River with Jeremiah Jones.

The man sensed Jim's need to know more. "Last I saw of him, Jed Mathews was with a bunch of them trapper fellers down in Santa Fe," he said finally. "They'd come down from Taos. They were talkin' about all the money they'd made last season trappin' and sellin' beaver pelts. Yer pa was listenin' real sharp. Talk is that he decided to go up to Taos with one of 'em. Kincaid—I think that was the feller's name."

"That would be David Kincaid. He and Pa knew each other when we stayed at Fort Kincaid."

Jim waited for further information, but none seemed to be forthcoming. The man was peering ahead toward the square and walking even faster. He seemed to have forgotten that he was not alone.

"Thank you, mister," Jim said. He stopped, letting the man go on his way. Then another question came to his mind. He ran after the red-bearded man again.

"Is he coming with the next caravan, mister? Do you know if he sent a letter with anyone?"

The man stopped. "Look, boy, I'd like to be able to tell you all about yer pa's plans, but I just don't know. I kind of think he had the itch to go with them trapper fellers, and when you go trappin', you go fer a whole season. Now you run along. Look fer some of yer pa's buddies. Maybe he sent word with them." This time Jim knew he had worn out the man's patience. He slowed his step and watched the man's back until the stranger reached the square.

What had he told him? Pa wasn't coming back? He wouldn't even be with the next caravan? Why would he break his promises? There just had to be word from him, so far away out there in the mountains! Pa wouldn't leave him without any word, no matter what!

The last thing Pa had said before he left was "Be watching for me, Jim-boy. I'll be back with the first caravan heading east. Then it's going to be like it should be—you and me together for always."

Without thinking where he was going, Jim turned off the main street, away from the crowds in the square and toward the Missouri River. Two short blocks brought him to the last of the log houses. The dark waters of the Missouri were beautiful now with the rosiness of sunset. Straight across the river, the bluffs on which the tiny village of Boonville stood were already dark. Someone in a cabin had placed a lighted candle in a window. The sight of it made Jim's throat tighten with the same kind of loneliness he had felt right after his pa left for Santa Fe.

He wanted to be alone awhile. The floods of last spring had brought logs ashore and left them on the gently sloping land along the river. Jim sat down on one now, facing the water. Two flatboats and a keelboat were tied at the river's edge. Usually there were boatmen around, but tonight the riverfront was deserted. He glanced behind him and to the left where the cigar factory, the ropewalk, and the warehouses stood. No one was around.

Jim turned back to the quiet river to try to think things through. What could have happened? His pa did strange things sometimes. Like two years ago after Jim's mother died of the fever. Pa had seemed even more lost than Jim, and for days he just sat on an old chair outside the cabin. Jim went to the tobacco field where the leaves were ripe, ready for cutting and drying. He came back and told Pa, "We've got to get that tobacco cut or it will be wasted."

But Pa just shook his head. The next morning Jim started to cut the crop himself. After the way they'd worked to keep the worms picked off—not to mention the work of plowing the good bottom field and setting out the young plants—it wouldn't be right just to let the leaves wither away!

Alone, Jim began the backbreaking job of cutting the leaves and tying them in bundles. He had most of the crop hung to dry in the tobacco barn when, one morning, Pa didn't go out and sit in front of the cabin. He cleaned his rifle, saddled up his horse, and said, "I'll be back, Jimboy."

Then he had ridden away.

When he was alone, Jim had let out the tears that a boy wasn't supposed to shed. Didn't Pa know that he was lonely too? Didn't he know that Jim missed his ma just as much as anybody?

The three of them had come to Missouri from Kentucky back when Jim was six years old. They had a little farm about five miles up the river, after the Indians had left and it was safe to move out of the forts. Pa had worked hard to build them a nice log house and to clear a field to plant crops.

When Mr. Bingham, who owned Franklin's Square and Compass Inn, opened the cigar factory on the riverfront, Jed Mathews was one of the first to have a crop of tobacco ready to sell.

Jim glanced over at the factory now. The last sunset glow reflected on its fine glass windows. He remembered the times he and Pa had brought in a wagon full of good tobacco leaves.

"Fine, fine," Mr. Bingham would say as he examined the crop, and Pa would near burst with pride. While the two men bargained for what the crop was worth, Jim and the Bingham boy, George Caleb, would go down to the dock. Caleb would forget he was supposed to be back at work in the factory, for he loved to draw pictures of the boats and boatmen. He would sketch away on a piece of shingle board as if it were paper. Jim had wondered how Caleb could do those pictures—they were really good. He could even draw the boatmen so they looked real.

But Mr. Bingham would call, "George Caleb Bingham! I thought you were inside packing cigars! Boy, if you spend your time drawing instead of working, you're never going to amount to anything!"

Jim smiled briefly, remembering how Caleb would tuck the board inside his shirt so he could finish the drawing first chance he had. Jim seldom saw Caleb these days, for now Caleb's father was dead, and Caleb had to spend most of his time working on the family farm a few miles upriver near Arrow Rock.

Sure miss old Caleb, Jim thought. He and Caleb used to talk about important things, such as what they'd do when they were grown men, what the world was like farther up the river, and who could throw a stone the farthest out over the Missouri. Yes, he sure missed Caleb. Kit was a good friend, too, but Caleb was special.

Loneliness swept over him again, and he came back to his thoughts about what had happened. Would Pa really go trapping without him, like the red-bearded man had said?

Old feelings of anger he had felt against his pa came back now as he sat there on the log. Why had he let him down again? The boy got up and began to walk toward the docks. It was nearly dark, and he had to watch his step to avoid tripping over the ropes that moored the flatboats. The river lapped against the rough boards of the boats and the gentle sounds quieted Jim's anger.

"Pa came back that time," he said aloud, "and he will again. He didn't forget me—he just has to go off by himself sometimes."

He remembered how, on the fifth day after his pa rode away from the cabin, he came riding back.

"Hello, Jim-boy," he had said in his old way. "Got some things to talk over with you."

They had planned it all then. They would get the tobacco to market and find work for Jim to do in Franklin.

"I'll sell the farm, Jim-boy, and in the spring I'll buy a stock of goods to take out to Santa Fe. I'll have five times as much money when I come back for you. Then you 'n' me will turn around and head west together. We can buy our outfit for trappin', and we'll be off to the rich beaver country. I heard Ewing Young is doin' real well since he left Franklin. He's got a kind of store in Taos, north of Santa Fe."

In the spring they had seen Mr. Hood's ad in *The Missouri Intelligencer*. He was looking for a boy to work for him.

"Just the place for you, Jim-boy," said Pa. "Robert Hood is not only a good merchant—he's also a good man."

Mr. Hood had looked Jim over carefully when Pa and Jim went to apply for the job.

"A might thin, but Mrs. Hood's cooking will fatten him up, I think. He'll do," the storekeeper had said. Jim looked down at his thin wrists, showing below the sleeves of his best jacket. He felt uncomfortable until he looked up and caught the twinkle in Mr. Hood's eyes.

Mr. Hood led the way to a room at the back of the store. "You'll sleep back here, Jim, in the storeroom. But our home will be yours, too, until your father gets back."

Jim's pa had been ready to leave two days later. A caravan was assembling in the square in Franklin. He had traded his saddle horse for a pair of good mules, and bought another pair as well. The farm wagon, which Pa said he would also sell in Santa Fe, was loaded with bolts of cloth from Mr. Hood's store, and supplies for the long journey. While they waited for the caravan to start, Pa and Jim sat together on the wagon seat.

"Son," Pa said, "I want to tell you a few things that are on my mind."

Jim waited for him to go on. Looking up, he saw that his father was having trouble speaking. Jim had never seen him cry except when they buried his mother. Now Pa rubbed a tear from his eye with the back of his hand. Then he spoke.

"Remember all your ma told you, Jim. Don't never forget she wanted more'n anythin' for you to grow up to be a fine upstandin' man—better'n me."

He stopped again. Then he went on. "Be true to all she taught you, Jim-boy. Think before you act, and keep that temper under control. Be honest, and always do what you know is right. She taught you that. Listen to that still voice inside you when you can't decide what you should do."

Then he cleared his throat. "You know what's right to do, Jim-boy, better'n I can say it. But I'll be back in the fall and we'll be together again. We'll head back west to be trappers. And if anythin' should happen to keep me out there—like if I broke a leg or somethin'—I'll get a message to you with someone who's coming back. I'll feel good knowin' that you are stayin' right here with Mr. Hood and his family."

Just then Pa's old friend Jeremiah Jones had come riding up. He had a string of pack mules all loaded for the trip.

"They're about ready to start, Jed."

Jim had grasped his father's hand for just a moment and then jumped down from the wagon. He remembered now how he couldn't look up at Pa, and how hard it had been to say, "See you when the caravan comes back." His throat had been so tight.

It was tight again now. He saw that it was almost dark and the river looked black. He turned back toward the square, suddenly remembering that Mrs. Hood would be wondering why he hadn't shown for supper.

The square was usually deserted at this time of the evening, but tonight it fairly glowed with lanterns and candles. Groups of men stood about the storefronts and on the grassy area where the wagons were drawn up.

Their voices lifted Jim's spirits. That red-bearded man could have been wrong. Maybe Pa was at the store after all—or at least there would be a message for him there. He quickened his steps.

3

Jim Sees Red

JIM was halfway across the square when he heard someone calling his name.

"Hey, Jim!" It was Kit, running toward him.

Kit was excited and couldn't seem to get the words out fast enough. "I found my brother William! You know what, Jim? William and Ham are both going out on the caravan that's leaving in two weeks—and I'm going too!"

"Gee, Kit—that's great! How did you get your ma and your stepfather to say you could go?"

Kit looked down at his dusty feet and wiped one of them on the leg of his pants. "Well . . . that's the only part that's not settled. I haven't been home yet to talk to them."

"Will Mr. Workman let you out of your apprenticeship?"

"I think so, if my stepfather asks him to."

"Well, you know enough now about saddle-making. That one you made for yourself is as good as any I ever saw. Come on with me. I've got to see if Pa is waiting for me at the store. Maybe we'll all go west together!"

The two started across the square toward Hood's store.

"I'm supposed to meet William at the Square and

Compass in about a half hour," Kit said. "I'm going out to the farm with him and Ham and Robert tonight. Mr. Workman said I could go."

The boys reached the wooden platform in front of the store and jumped up from the dusty street. It was after the usual closing time, but the oil lamps and some candles had been lighted for this special evening. Mr. Hood was standing in the open doorway.

"Where've you been, boy?" he asked. Then he sighed. "No need to tell me, Jim. You've been with your pa. How is he?"

Jim stopped short. Pa wasn't here. He swallowed hard before he asked, "Did anyone come here with a message for me, Mr. Hood? I haven't found Pa, and one fellow said he didn't think he came back."

Mr. Hood shook his head. "No, Jim. A fellow did come here with this saddle and saddlebags, but that's all."

He pointed to some dusty leather things heaped on the boards beside him.

"Whose are they?" Kit asked.

"Fellow named Clarkson brought them, but he said they belonged to Jeremiah Jones. He said Jones had ridden ahead of the caravan one day, trying to get to the Cimarron River to see if it had water or had gone dry. When the rest of them reached the Cimarron, they found Jones lying there. He was almost dead, with an arrow in his back. He bent over him, Clarkson said, and Jones whispered something about taking these things to Hood's in Franklin."

Kit, taking an interest in the saddle, lifted it and wiped away some of the dust with his shirttail. "It's beautiful. Looks like that fancy kind they make in Mexico."

"Did Clarkson say anything else?" Jim asked.

"Just that after they buried poor Jeremiah, he packed up this gear and hauled it along. I guess someone in Jones's family will come along and pick it up one of these days."

"Jeremiah didn't have any family that I know of, Mr. Hood," Jim said. "He was Pa's best friend. He used to come out to our farm, and he and Pa would go hunting together. I'm sure sorry he was killed."

"Do you s'pose Jeremiah was going to bring you word about your pa?" Kit asked.

"Likely he was," Jim said. "Pa would have sent word to me with Jeremiah for sure." He turned his head away so that Kit and Mr. Hood wouldn't see him blink back the tears. "Sure wish I knew what happened. . . ."

Mr. Hood put an arm around Jim's shoulder. "Cheer up, Jim. There's hardly been enough time for a man to get the saddle off his mule. Likely your pa will show up any minute."

Jim shook his head. "I don't think so, Mr. Hood. I met a man who said he didn't think Pa came back with the caravan. Said he hadn't seen him since they left Santa Fe."

Mr. Hood looked surprised. "That's strange. I should think he'd have seen every man that was traveling in the caravan some time or other."

"That's not it, Mr. Hood. He said Pa didn't even start out. He heard him talking about going up to Taos to go beaver-trapping."

Kit had been examining the saddle carefully. Now he put it down and said, "If he did that, Jim, he'd sure enough send you a message. He wouldn't just leave you wondering what happened."

"Well, let's not just stand here wondering about it," Mr. Hood said. "Come on in, boys, and please bring in that saddle and those saddlebags. Put them back in the corner behind the wagon wheels. They'll be safe there till someone comes for them. Mrs. Hood saved a pot pie for you, Jim. She had me bring it back here when you didn't show up for supper."

"Thanks," Jim said. He picked up the saddlebags, which were obviously much older and more worn than the saddle. Kit was already carrying the saddle back to the rear of the store.

As they put down Jeremiah's belongings, Kit said, "I'll wait for you while you eat your supper, Jim. After you eat, come on over to the Square and Compass with me. My brothers might know something more about your pa."

"Would that be all right, Mr. Hood?" Jim asked. "I won't stay over there long." He noticed that his broom and apron had been put back in their proper places. *Mr. Hood must be expecting me to go on working as usual,* he thought as he picked up the warm pot pie from the counter.

Mr. Hood had gone over to the other side of the store. "Yes, Jim, you can go, but don't stay out late. There'll be some pretty rough fellows around the square tonight— rougher than usual after they get through celebrating. I'll lock up the store now, so you be careful. It's a warm night, but you'd best close the back door and put the bar in place."

"Yes, sir," Jim said.

"I'll go on home now," said Mr. Hood. "Kit, come and help me bar the front door."

The wooden-slab door had an iron lock on it, and Mr. Hood turned the key. Then he and Kit lowered a heavy piece of oak about two inches thick and five feet long into L-shaped braces set into either side of the door frame. Kit went back to sit beside Jim as Mr. Hood snuffed out the candles and one of the two hanging oil lamps.

"You can put out the other lamp before you go, boys. And don't let anyone in the store for any reason. Good night. Try to be back here by nine o'clock, Jim."

Mr. Hood went back through the storeroom that was Jim's bedroom and closed the bottom half of the split door behind him. Kit, waiting for Jim to finish the last of his squirrel pie, was gazing about at the strange shadows made by the swaying oil lamp.

"Did you ever look at the shadows from that stuff hanging up there?" he asked. "Looks like bears and ghosts and all sorts of things."

Jim looked at the log walls and the open spaces above the long beams, from which hung tinware, some wooden buckets, a few hickory-splint baskets, and an assortment of harness pieces. There was even a pair of gentlemen's city shoes hanging there, and a pair of high-lacing ladies' shoes to go with them.

"Looks like a man and lady ghost out for a walk over there," he said. "I don't like to be here alone when the lamps are lit. I'd rather just carry a candle when I have to come in here in the dark."

"I don't blame you," Kit said. "It gives me the shivers. If it didn't smell right, I'd think I wasn't in a store at all."

Jim swallowed the last bit of his supper. "I kind of like the smell now that I'm used to it. Lots of things all mixed together—vinegar, old leather, tea leaves, coffee beans, and those wooden wine and beer kegs. Anyway, I'm done now. Let's go over to Bingham's. There's probably a big crowd there."

Most people still called the Square and Compass "Bingham's" because Caleb's father had owned it. The Bingham family lived there when they first came to Franklin from the East. Jim had always liked to go there whenever Pa and Ma and he came into town from the farm. Sometimes they'd sat down at the big table in the public room and had their noon meal from the steaming platters and bowls that Mrs. Bingham set out for the customers each day. Caleb had waited on tables, even though he wasn't very big, until his father opened the cigar factory. Then he'd had to help down there most of the time.

The boys crossed the square. Bingham's was at the northwest corner, and they had to make their way around several groups of men standing and sitting outside the shops, stores, and other taverns. They reached the doorway of the inn and saw that the place was crowded. The heavy wooden door hung open to let in the warm night air.

"How are you going to find William in this crowd?" Jim yelled into Kit's ear, for the place was noisy with loud voices, shuffling feet, and clattering pottery and tinware. "It's a good thing your brothers aren't short like you!"

Just then, a cheerful voice rose over the hubbub, and a boy about their own age, wearing an apron and carrying a tray as if it were a shield, came pushing through the crowd. "Kit! Jim!"

"Hey, it's old Caleb!" Kit said. "Back workin' like he used to!"

Caleb Bingham's smile was almost as wide as his round face under curly dark hair. His brown eyes almost always sparkled, and now they lighted up his whole face. He looked for a place where his two friends could sit. They didn't get many chances to see each other now that all three of them had reached the age where a boy was expected to spend most of his time working. Like Jim, Caleb was fifteen.

"There's just one place left to sit down," he said. "Over on the stairway with some of the other boys. Maybe I can come and sit with you awhile when things let up a bit."

They made their way through the crowd to the wide stairway that led to the second floor, where the sleeping rooms were. Caleb followed them, and Jim turned back long enough to yell into his ear, "Have you seen my father? I'm trying to find him."

For some reason, the place quieted just as Jim was speaking, and he was embarrassed to hear himself yelling in the sudden lull. Several heads turned toward the boys, then turned back to their conversations.

"No, Jim," Caleb said quietly, "I haven't seen him since the day the caravan left for Santa Fe." He glanced over to where the fiddler, the night's entertainment, was still tuning up, and then added, "But I don't get to town very often now that my mother needs me to help at the farm."

"Boy! Fill up these mugs!" someone called, and Caleb hurried away. The noise of the crowd was building again, and the fiddling could hardly be heard above it. Jim saw that Kit was climbing the stairs to an open space, making his way with difficulty because the steps were crowded with boys and young men.

He was about to follow Kit when he noticed that Coy Colton was sprawled on the first step, his elbows on the second and his long legs stretched out in front of him. He was taking up twice as much space as any other person in the group.

I'll pretend I don't even know he's there, Jim told himself, but the tingling feel of blood rushing to his head came to him anyway.

As he stepped between Coy's elbow and the banister, there was a sudden pressure against his right leg. He looked down and saw that Coy was pushing his leg with his foot, trying to make him lose his balance. Jim tried to grab the stair post to steady himself, but he fell over onto Tom Fuller, sitting one step up. Tom was apprenticed to a cabinetmaker who had a shop near Hood's store. He and Jim were friends.

"Hey, that's no way to do, Jim," Tom said, laughing. "I'd have let you through!"

"Sorry, Tom," said Jim, getting his balance back. He nodded his head toward Coy. "There's a guy here with awful big feet and bad manners."

"I heard that, Beanpole," Coy said. He turned on the stair and thrust his right leg in front of Tom, blocking the way as much as he could. There was no way Jim could get up the stairs.

Jim turned an angry look on Coy. Small eyes above a yellow-toothed grin met his gaze.

"What's the matter, little boy?" Coy's voice was syrupy and mocking. "Can't find your daddy? I heard you asking about him—he's not here. But don't cry, little boy."

That voice, dripping sweet, was more than Jim could bear. Looking at Tom, he said, "He's not only got big feet—he's got a big mouth, too."

"Shut up, you dumb beanpole." Coy's mocking grin had disappeared. "You can't talk to me like that!" His voice was angry now. "I don't blame your pa for not coming back. Who'd want a dumb kid like you that can't even climb up some steps?"

Jim froze. "Easy, Jim," Tom said to him softly. "He's a lot bigger and meaner than you are."

But Jim had had all he could take. "And a lot dumber, too," he said, loud enough for Coy to hear.

The blood rushed in Jim's ears and made him unable to hear the sounds around him. He felt the thrust of Coy's foot once again, and this time the big, dirty toes hit his ribs. Jim's long right arm shot out and found its target. Blood spurted from Coy's nose. Coy was too surprised to do anything but put up his hand to try to stop the flow.

From his perch up the stairs, Kit yelled, "Oh, Jim! You're in for it now!"

Quickly, Kit took hold of the stair rail and vaulted over it, landing in a clear spot on the floor below. People made room for him as he lunged toward Jim.

"Come on, you crazy hothead," he said as he pulled at Jim's left arm. "Come on, before that big ox gets on his feet. He'll grind you up like they grind flour at the mill!"

Jim stood without moving, resisting the pull of Kit's hands. He was so angry that it was several seconds before he saw the blood on Coy's face. It came to him then that he'd better get moving.

Coy was struggling to his feet, and with the crowd of people to get through, it looked as if there'd be no chance for Jim to escape. Kit tugged hard at Jim's arm when he saw Coy get up. Then his view was suddenly blocked by the back of a big serving tray. Caleb had pushed his way between Jim and Coy. "Get going," he whispered to Jim.

Then Caleb said, "Oh—sorry, Coy," as he stumbled over him and pushed him back onto the steps, falling with the tray onto Coy's lap.

The last Jim heard was Coy yelling, "Get out of my way, you little pipsqueak! Let me at that Mathews! I'll fix him for sure!"

But Kit and Jim were already at the back door of the inn. Both boys had spent many hours in this building, and they knew their way well. They went through a dark storage room and out to the inn yard.

They picked their way carefully, for the yard was full of wagons and gear left by the men stopping at the inn. Beyond were stables, and the boys made their way past them to a gate that led to a dark side street. They hurried on down the street, away from the lighted town square.

"Thanks, Kit," Jim said when they were far enough away from the inn to slow down to a walk. "You saved me from a real beating."

Kit was out of breath. "You've gotta learn to hold your temper, Jim," he said when he could talk. "If Caleb hadn't helped you out, I hate to think what you'd look like now!"

"I know. But every time I see that Coy, he makes my blood boil. I guess I really saw red this time. It was a stupid thing to do."

They walked on, looking back often to see if Coy and his friends were following.

"Seems safe so far," Kit said. "But if I know that guy, he'll be after you. You head for Hood's the long way 'round, and I'll go back to Bingham's. I'm sure I saw William when we were rushin' out. I'm ridin' home with him tonight, but I'll be back in tomorrow. Take it easy now!" He started to walk away and then turned back. "Hey, Jim, tomorrow's Saturday. Are you goin' to the racetrack?"

"I think so. Mr. Hood said he was closing up the store early 'cause everybody'd be out at the races. He told me I could go, too. Are you going?"

"I'm gonna try to. Well—see you there then. So long!"

"So long, Kit—and thanks again."

Jim stayed a block north of the square until he reached the Hoods' house. It was directly behind the store, facing onto the next street. All the lights were out, and Jim walked quietly through the backyard to the rear of the store. As he passed the stable and carriage house, he was glad for the moonlight. Mr. Hood used most of the yard space for storage, so there were empty barrels stacked two or three high. There were also some log poles lying alongside two wagons.

Jim picked his way carefully until he reached the door that led into the storeroom. He had left the upper half of the door open earlier for ventilation, closing the lower half to keep animals out. Now he went inside, closed both halves of the door, and dropped the bar into place, remembering his promise to Mr. Hood.

"Guess I'll just go to bed without lighting a candle," he said aloud. Moonlight shone into the little room through a square window above his bed, which was just a wooden frame resting on two legs and on pegs driven into the log wall. Ropes laced back and forth across the bed to support a mattress of homespun material stuffed with corn shucks. Beside his bed, next to the door, an upended box served as a night table.

The rest of the room, except for a small trunk that had belonged to Jim's mother, held only boxes, kegs, and barrels. These were filled with merchandise ready to be taken out to the front of the store when they were needed. Over the bed hung Jim's long Kentucky rifle and his powder horn, and a shelf on which were a few of his personal things, such as his extra shirt and trousers, bullets, wadding, and a ramrod for his rifle.

Mr. Hood had cautioned Jim about the boxes in the storeroom, especially the ones marked EXPLOSIVES. "Be careful in moving any of those," he said. "As you can see, some of them contain gunpowder. We'll keep them back near the wall, out of your way. These heavy ones beside the door are full of bar lead for bullets, and these long boxes hold rifles."

Tired, Jim stretched out on the mattress. The little room was hot with the door closed. Some air came between the logs where chinking had fallen out, but not enough to make the room comfortable. He turned first to one side and then to the other, but he could not get to sleep.

Sure would like to open the top half of that door, he thought. *But if I did and anything happened, it would be my own fault.*

Things seemed to have quieted down outside. Jim got up and peered through the window. The barrels in the backyard were clearly outlined, and beyond them rose an old sycamore tree. The leaves of the tree began to dance in a slight breeze, but none of it cooled his room.

Sighing, he lay down again. Every sound in the store seemed extra-loud in the stillness of the night. On his first night in the storeroom, Jim had been a little frightened of those sounds—the creaking of floorboards, of course, but also the scurrying of small feet and the gnawing sounds, too.

"Just can't keep out the field mice when you have a store on the frontier," Mr. Hood had told him. "They can always find a way to get to the bits of grain and flour and sugar we spill."

Sometimes there were more frightening noises from outside. One night Jim had heard the yowl of a wildcat, near enough to leap through the upper half of the door, had it been open. Another night, there had been the sound of some of the barrels being knocked over. The next morning, Jim and Mr. Hood had found bear tracks out there. Jim was glad to have his rifle with him in the storeroom. He might have to use it some night!

This night there were other sounds. The shouting and music were still going on at the taverns on the other side of the square, and there were sounds of horses' hooves thudding on the dusty street as men rode off at last to their lodgings. The noises grew less and less, and Jim found himself several times on the verge of falling asleep when an extra-loud shout would bring him back to wakefulness again.

He lay there feeling lonely and wondering about his pa. Could he really have gone trapping beaver *without* him? Surely he would have sent word. Or maybe he had, and it died with Jeremiah Jones out on the Cimarron—

Then suddenly he was wide awake. Someone was knocking on the front door of the store.

4

Night Visitors

JIM'S first thought was of his father. Maybe he was in Franklin after all and had been delayed for some reason back down the trail a ways. Jim got up and started toward the front of the store in the dark, for there was no time to light a candle. The knocking came again.

When he was near enough to the front door, he called out, "Who's there?"

His heart was pounding as he listened for the answer, but the voice he heard was not his father's.

"Jim Mathews! Come and open the door!" There was quiet for a moment, and Jim tried to think who could be out there. Then the voice said, "I've come all the way from Santa Fe and I'm tired. If you don't want this letter badly enough to open up, I'm goin' on home."

Suddenly Jim realized he was shaking. Excitement welled up within him; news from Pa! He knew Pa wouldn't leave him without word!

"I'm coming!" he called, but it was so dark in the store he had to grope his way carefully toward the front.

"Make it fast!" the voice called impatiently.

Then someone else spoke in lower tones, and the first speaker said something in reply that Jim couldn't hear. He

33

was almost to the door and about to try to lift the bar when he remembered he didn't have a key for the lock. Mr. Hood had taken the key with him.

Mr. Hood's words came back to Jim, just as if he were standing there now. "Don't let anyone in the store for any reason."

"Can you slip the letter under the door?" Jim called out. "I don't have a key to unlock it."

"No. It's a thick packet. Come on, kid. I can't stand here all night gabbing. Let me in or I'll just take this on home with me and leave it up to you to find out where it is."

"Please—just a minute," Jim said. "I'll use the back door. I'll be around in just a minute."

"Well . . . all right, but make it fast."

He turned to go back to the storeroom, but a sudden thought stopped him. That voice—where had he heard it before? And why hadn't whoever had that letter sent it over earlier, before the store closed for the night? An uneasy feeling came over Jim. Best be careful.

He reached the little back room. It sounded as if the visitors, whoever they were, were alongside the building in the alley that led to the backyard. Again, Mr. Hood's caution came to mind.

Getting up on the bed, Jim pressed his face against the glass of the small window, hoping to get a glimpse of whoever was out there. No one was in sight, but he heard footsteps coming around the corner of the building to his left. Then he heard a laugh, and the laugh sounded all too familiar.

The voice spoke again, this time just outside the door. "Open up, kid. We haven't got all night."

The voice was different now, as if the speaker had been trying to disguise it and was not being as careful as he had at first. Jim watched as two shadowy forms came into view—boys, a little smaller than Kit.

And then he knew there was no letter from his father. The fellow at the door could be no one else but Coy.

"You'll have to leave the packet on the barrel," he called out. "I'll get it in the morning. I can't get the bar off this door. But thanks for bringing the letter over."

Now the voice dropped its disguise entirely. "Come on, kid. Open that door and hurry up about it."

"Go home, Coy Colton," Jim called loudly. "I know what you want. Now get out of here and get out fast. I've got a rifle in here and I'll use it." Jim knew he couldn't make good on this threat, for his gun was not loaded, and he didn't even have the powder and shot he'd need to get it ready to fire. He hadn't used it since he went hunting with Pa last winter.

"You ain't got no rifle, Beanpole. We're comin' in!"

He peered out the window again. Coy, dressed in his dusty clothes, had stepped into full view in the moonlight. Now he was backing off, as if getting ready to throw his full weight against the door. His two smaller friends looked ready to hold Jim down while Coy pounded him.

"What a beating I'll get if he breaks down the door!" Jim muttered. The heavy bar, positioned diagonally, braced both halves of the door, but just the same the planks could split.

Coy's shoulder hit the door with a heavy thud, and one board buckled a bit. Jim heard the screech of nails as they gave way a little. The door held, but he knew the upper half wouldn't last through many more blows. What could he do? If only Mr. Hood and he had rigged up that signal cord with a bell they had talked about!

Jim peered out the window again. Coy was bent over, holding his shoulder. He seemed to have hurt himself. There was a little time. He studied the boxes full of lead bars—they were too heavy for him to carry, but he dragged one over against the door. There was an iron crowbar by the wall, and by using it he was able to pry up the end of another box. He got a good grip on it and stacked it on top of the first box, but he knew he couldn't lift another high enough.

The rifles! The boxes were long. He stood two on end, leaning them against the upper half of the door. He dragged over another lead box to wedge them in place. Then he rolled a full whiskey barrel against the boxes. Not too bad a barricade, he thought.

Perspiration had soaked through his shirt. He climbed back up onto the bed to look out the window. No one was in sight in the moonlit yard. Had they given up that easily?

"Nope!" he said aloud. They wouldn't quit that soon.

"I'll get you some other time, Jim Mathews!" Coy called in his natural voice. "You can't poke me in the nose and get away with it, you dumb beanpole. We're goin' now, but you just watch out for me from here on, and don't try anythin' else."

Silence followed that speech. Jim listened for the sound of footsteps alongside the building. He heard none.

They're just trying to make me think they're leaving, Jim told himself. He'd get ready for the next attack. Then another idea came to him—an added surprise in case the barricade didn't hold.

He was glad of the moonlight, and that he knew his way around the store very well. Just around the corner in the front room was a big tin of pepper, which was kept on a low shelf. He found the tin and carried it back into the storeroom.

Mr. Hood won't like this . . . pepper comes high, he said to himself, *but I'll work extra hard to pay for it if I have to use it.* He loosened the lid of the pepper tin and set the box on his bed. He could easily get a handful to throw if he should have to. Then he took his rifle from the wall. At least he could use the stock end to strike out. He was as ready as he could be.

It was time to check the callers again. He peered out the window. The moonlight showed clearly what plan the three had worked out. They were picking up the heaviest of the cedar poles that lay in the yard.

Jim knew the door could not hold against the ramming of that pole. Even his barricade would be no good. If only Mr. Hood would realize what was going on! Jim could blind Coy with the pepper and gain a little time, but that would only make the big guy angrier. He had a sinking feeling. What should he do?

Coy's loud whisper interrupted his thoughts.

"Ready, boys—all together—no, wait a minute! Back up farther so's we can get a better run!"

A second later there was a great clatter and rumbling. Some barrels stacked in the yard had tumbled down. Coy cursed. He and his pals had backed up without looking to see where the end of the pole reached.

"Oh! My foot!" one of the smaller boys yelled.

"Shut up! You'll have the whole town on us!" Coy hissed.

Then came another voice. "What's going on there?"

Mr. Hood! The yelling and clatter had awakened him. Robert Hood, in his nightshirt and slippers, came into view in the yard, his rifle in his hand. Jim had never been happier to see him.

Coy and his friends dropped the pole, and Jim could hear the thudding of their feet as they ran through the alley alongside the store.

"Get off my land or I'll shoot!" Mr. Hood shouted.

There was another yowl of pain. Somebody stubbed his toe, Jim figured.

Mr. Hood followed the intruders a short way, then came to the back door. "Are you all right, Jim?"

"Yes, sir. Just scared. I've got things stacked behind the door, but I sure was glad to see you."

"Want me to spend the night in the store?"

"No, sir. I don't think those guys'll dare come back again tonight, but I'll just leave these things stacked until morning."

"Good night, then. Glad you remembered not to open up. You can tell me what happened tomorrow."

Morning came too soon for Jim. It seemed to him that he had just fallen into an uneasy sleep when daylight awoke him. The room was stuffy with yesterday's air, and Jim's head was filled all too soon with yesterday's problems.

He turned on his side and saw the barricade he'd built. The first job of this hot day would be to take it down. The day should have been the joyful beginning of the new life he and Pa planned to share. Instead, he not only didn't know where his father was but also had to worry about what Coy Colton would do next.

He got up and began by moving the barrel to its original place, rolling it back to the other side of the room. Next, he struggled with the heavy boxes of rifles. *Coy sure is a nuisance,* he thought. *He makes me mad.* Jim gave a box of lead an extra-hard shove and added a kick for good measure. Now his toe hurt too. As he stood on one foot, holding the toe that was the victim of his anger, he remembered how his mother used to scold him. "Use your head, Jim! Your temper won't solve your problem, and you'll only get into trouble."

If I'd held my temper last night, he told himself now, *I wouldn't have to move all this stuff!* He struggled with the last box of lead, trying to get it back where Mr. Hood had placed it. He was already wet with sweat, and he still had to hoist the bar off its rests.

Finally, he swung open both parts of the back door and stepped outside. The sky had the pale look of a warm day, with no promise of the much-needed rain.

"Sure going to be hot out at the races this afternoon," he said aloud.

"Who are you talking to, young man?" It was Mr. Hood, ready to go into the store and unlock it for the day's business.

Jim grinned. "To my best listener—myself. I've been telling myself that I sure messed things up last night."

"Just exactly what happened? I thought you seemed rather upset about your father last night, but that couldn't possibly bring on an attack by a bunch of rough-necks."

"No, sir. You know that big guy that works at the flour mill—Coy Colton? Well, he's got it in for me for some reason. Last night over at Bingham's he tried to block my way. Then he said something about my pa and me. I was so mad I just struck out at him and hit him a good one in the nose."

"You hit a guy twice your size? What was that sup-posed to accomplish?"

Jim was washing himself from a bucket of water that stood on a bench along the back wall of the building, splashing water over his face and hair.

"Coy was sitting on the bottom step," Jim went on, "leaning back and off-balance when I did it. It was a lucky punch, that's all. Anyway, he called me a 'dumb bean-pole,' and I guess he was right."

Mr. Hood shook his head. "It was pretty stupid to strike a fellow as big and mean as that," he said. Then, seeing the unhappy expression on Jim's face, he laid a hand on the boy's shoulders and spoke more sympatheti-cally. "So that's why we had night callers?"

"Yes, sir. I'm awfully sorry. And I'm glad they didn't do any more damage than to mess up the yard and crack that one board in the door. I'll clean it all up. I guess Coy has a sore shoulder this morning."

Mr. Hood started into the store. Jim followed him, carrying the box of pepper to put it back on the shelf. Mr. Hood didn't ask him what he'd been doing with it. All he said was "Mrs. Hood says you should go eat your breakfast. She worries about you—thinks you're too thin. Get going now."

A few minutes later, Jim was sitting at the big table in the combination kitchen–sitting room of the Hood house. Mrs. Hood put cornbread, bacon, and a pitcher of milk in front of him.

When Jim had been eating for a few minutes, she came and sat down across from him. "Now tell me what's been going on," she said. To Mrs. Hood, who had no children of her own, the boy was more like a son every day. Jim looked on her almost as he would his own mother.

"I thought for sure Pa would be with the men who came back from Santa Fe yesterday," Jim said. "But he wasn't. And so far I haven't had any word from him."

"Who would be most likely to bring you the message?"

"Jeremiah Jones. He was Pa's closest friend, and he started back with the caravan. But he was killed out at the Cimarron River crossing." Jim paused. "If Jeremiah was supposed to give me a message, I'll never know what it was."

Mrs. Hood reached out and touched his hand. "Would there be anyone else?" she asked.

Jim shook his head. "I can't think of anyone else. Pa knew Kit's brother William from when we all stayed at Fort Kincaid—but William hasn't said anything to me about Pa. And another man said that Pa was thinking about going up to Taos to trap beaver. I don't know what to think."

"Well, Jim," Mrs. Hood said confidently, "you'll hear from your father soon. He thinks too much of you to just go off in the mountains trapping without sending some word. You know that. Cheer up!" She got up and went around the table to give Jim's shoulders a reassuring hug.

Jim felt the lump that hurt so much coming back into his throat. He tried to swallow some cornbread, but it stuck, and he choked and coughed. Mrs. Hood poured some milk and Jim drank some of it. When he could speak again, he said, "I don't know if he'll ever come back."

"Come on, now! You know better than that! He'll come back for you. You just hold on and you'll hear from him. And in the meantime, you know you have a home and a family right here as long as you need it. First thing you know, you'll be heading west, too, and much as I hate the idea, I'll be having to say good-bye to you."

Jim felt better. Suddenly an idea came to him, and an eager look came to his face.

"Mrs. Hood!" he said excitedly. "A man brought Jeremiah's saddle and saddlebags back to the store. Maybe there's something for me in the saddlebags!"

"Of course! There probably is!"

Jim had finished his breakfast by this time, and he jumped up. "Excuse me. I'm going to the store right now to check!"

"I'll be wanting to know if you find anything—and remember, Jim, anytime you need someone to talk to, I'm here!"

Jim hurried back to the store.

"Mr. Hood, I want to look in Jeremiah's saddlebags and see if there's anything in them for me before I start work, if that's all right."

He was already pulling the old leather bags from the corner when Mr. Hood answered, "Good idea, Jim—but I will need you in just a few minutes. Tom Fuller is coming over to watch the store for a while—they're not busy over at the cabinet shop, and I need you with me to look over the animals the men brought from Santa Fe."

"Yes, sir—just a minute." Jim had the saddlebags pulled out from behind the wagon wheels. He unbuckled one side and reached into the pocket. He couldn't see very well there in the shadowy back of the store, but most of the things he recognized by feel. There was a bundle of bits of cotton cloth—wadding that Jeremiah used to load his rifle—a heavy bar of lead, a bullet mold and a sack of bullets, a piece of leather, and an awl. These were the miscellaneous things that a man wouldn't hang from his belt. Jim decided that this pocket was not the one in which a letter for him would be stored, but he felt around some more to make sure.

He closed that half of the bag just as Tom arrived. Quickly, he unbuckled the other side. It held Jeremiah's extra clothing, and Jim impatiently pulled out a pair of trousers to see what was under them. He found a pair of hand-knitted socks and some Indian moccasins. Under those he saw a shirt.

"Jim, Mr. Patton wants Tom back at his shop by noon, so we'd better get started," Mr. Hood called out. Tom was apprenticed to the cabinetmaker who had a shop next to the store, and from time to time he was allowed to help Mr. Hood when there was no piece of work on which Mr. Patton needed assistance.

"Yes, sir. Be there in a minute," Jim called.

Tom had strolled back to where Jim was crouched over the saddlebags. "You were lucky to get away last night," he said. "Boy, was Coy mad! He gave Caleb a shove that sent him over backwards, but Caleb managed to get in his way again. He did everythin' he could to give you more time, you know. Did Coy catch up with you? You don't look like you got beat up."

"I didn't—not last night. But he's still after me, I know that much."

Jim was on his knees, groping in the bottom of the pocket. Tom looked him over.

"You're right. I'd hate to be in your shoes," Tom said. "It's all over town now that Coy Colton is sore as a boil. He's telling everyone that he's gonna give you the beatin' of your life."

Jim felt prickles at the back of his neck. What a fool he'd been! But to Tom he said, "What was I supposed to do—just grin and take that stuff from him?"

"I think I would've," Tom said. "He's so mean I'd have changed my mind right off about goin' up those steps. It wouldn't have made you seem like a coward to back off— just a guy with some good sense."

Mr. Hood called from near the front door, "Enough chatter, boys. If any big buyer comes in, Tom, hold him for me until I get back. Come on, Jim. I'll start out, and you can catch up."

"I'll talk to you later, Tom." Jim took one final feel around the contents of the bag, shoved the trousers back in, and put the bags back in the corner.

"No letter here," he sighed. "Thought maybe Jeremiah might have a letter from my pa in his saddlebags, but I guess not."

"Maybe it was in the pocket of the clothes he had on," Tom said.

This was not a cheerful thought to Jim, but he had no time to dwell on it. If the message was in one of Jeremiah's pockets, it had most likely gone into the grave with him.

Jim hurried out the front door and ran to catch up to his employer.

"Guess you didn't find a letter," Mr. Hood said.

"No, sir."

"Well, while you're waiting to hear from your father, we'll have lots to do. I want to buy up some animals before the choice ones are gone. I'm going to need your help, first in choosing the best stock, and then in taking care of them until we sell them. This afternoon we'll saddle up a couple of mules and get someone to help us herd the animals out to my pasture lot."

"Yes, sir. That'll be fine." Jim was trying to keep his mind off his own problems and was glad there was work to do. But he wondered if Mr. Hood had forgotten that he'd given Jim permission to go to the races and the goose pull. The events started at about three o'clock, and everyone in town closed up their stores and shops to join the crowd out at the track.

As if he could read Jim's thoughts, Mr. Hood said, "You can take one of the mules and use him in the goose pull if you want to, Jim. We'll be through before the races start."

Out at the sale lot, they looked over the mules. Jim had learned from his father how to judge a mule: one looked for sturdy legs, a broad chest, and bright eyes. Settlers on the Missouri farms found mules better than horses for pulling plows, and traders going west wanted them for freight wagons.

"Maybe you and I will go into the mule business, Jim," Mr. Hood said. He was obviously enjoying himself. "We can raise them ourselves. Let's take about ten of these Mexican burros, along with the fifty mules I'll try to sell."

As they herded the animals they wanted to buy into a corral, Jim considered Mr. Hood's remarks. *Seems like he's planning on my being around for quite a while,* he thought. *That's not such a good thing, 'cause I'm going west for sure— maybe even with Kit in a couple of weeks.* But he said nothing to Mr. Hood.

The morning was almost over, and it was time for the noon dinner when they got back to the store. Mr. Hood locked up for the day—everyone would be at the racetrack this Saturday afternoon—but before they left, he said to Jim, "Bring along Jones's saddle, Jim. It will be good for the leather if it's used, and you can use it this afternoon."

Jeremiah must have been right proud when he bought this saddle, Jim said to himself as he picked it up. He fingered the beautifully shaped and hammered silver ornaments on the skirt, and traced the intricate tooled pattern that formed a border on the leather. He wondered if Pa had been with Jeremiah when he picked it out.

Jim carried the saddle out to the wagon in the backyard and put it into the wagon box. After dinner he went back out to the yard to prepare for the afternoon events. Mr. Hood kept a team of horses in the stable most of the time, handy for trips out to his farm at the edge of town, or down to his warehouse at the riverfront. Jim found a saddle blanket, cinch, and bridle for the mule he would be riding later and put them into the wagon with the saddle. Then he busied himself at harnessing the team. He was backing the horses to the wagon tongue when Mr. Hood came out and added his gear to Jim's.

"Let's go," Mr. Hood said. "I've hired two hands to meet us at the sale lot. I think the four of us can herd the animals all right, don't you?"

"Yes, sir. And I've brought along a bell for the mare. Pa told me those Mexican mules are trained to follow a bell mare, and that would help us get them safely over to your farm."

When Jim had the last strap in place, he handed the reins to Mr. Hood on the wagon seat. In a moment he was up beside him.

"I'd like to ride Pedro this afternoon, if it's all the same to you, sir," Jim said as they came near the farm pasture lot. They would leave the wagon there and ride to the sale lot on mules.

"All right with me. You and Pedro seem to get along together just fine."

Soon Jim was putting the bridle, blanket, and saddle in place on Pedro, a sleek black mule he had ridden before. He had to shorten the stirrups only a little.

"Guess I must be nearly as tall as Jeremiah," he said to Mr. Hood, who was already mounted. "Pa will be really surprised at how much I've grown!"

It didn't take long to ride over to the sale lot. With the help of the two men who were waiting there, the mules and burros were soon on their way to the Hood pastures north of town. They were quite near the Franklin race-track, and Jim could see that people were already arriving for the afternoon's sport.

As Mr. Hood secured the pasture gate, he said, "I'll take the wagon back home and get Mrs. Hood. You and Pedro go and join your friends at the track. And oh, Jim, I'm hoping you'll join the goose pull. That's one reason I thought you should use that good saddle. It's just for fellows under twenty today, and you'd stand a good chance to win, I think."

Jim shook his head. "If it was a mule race, I'd enter, Mr. Hood. But I kind of don't like the idea of the goose pull."

Mr. Hood looked surprised. "I thought for sure you'd try for that goose. Mrs. Hood was hoping to roast it for our Sunday dinner tomorrow. Well, do as you like. We'll see you later. Have a good time."

He went on, but Jim could see that he was disappointed. As the wagon rumbled away and Jim turned Pedro toward the racetrack, someone called his name. It was Kit, riding double behind William. They drew alongside and Kit jumped down. William rode on to tie his horse to the track fence, in the shade of a tree.

"Where'd you get the dandy saddle?" asked Kit. Then he recognized it. "Oh, that's Jones's Mexican saddle, isn't it? Sure is a beauty." He examined the stitching with the critical eye of one who knows how a saddle should be made.

"Mr. Hood said he thought I should use it sometimes."

Kit was admiring the decorative tooling and the silver ornaments. "Those Mexicans sure do know how to make a beautiful saddle. Mine is stitched and padded as nice, but it don't have none of this fancy trimmin'."

Kit walked alongside Pedro as they went toward the track gates. "Hey, Jim, look who's comin'. It's your girlfriend."

Getting out of a carriage stopped at the gate were Martha and Dr. and Mrs. Lowry. Martha saw the boys and, after waving to her parents, walked over to them. "Are either of you going in the goose pull after the races?" she asked.

"I can't," Kit said. "Haven't got a mule to ride, and besides, I'm too short to get a good grip on the goose's neck."

Martha looked at Jim. "You're tall enough," she said. "And I see Mr. Hood let you ride Pedro. Do you think you'll enter? I sure would if I was a boy."

Jim was dismounting. "You would, Martha? I saw a goose pull last year and it didn't look like much fun to me. Twisting a goose's neck 'till its head comes off seems kind of cruel."

"Well, I guess it is," Martha said, "but everyone seems to think it's good sport. And you could do it just as well as any boy here, Jim—someone's going to do it, anyway."

Jim was looping Pedro's reins around the outer rail of the racetrack when Martha noticed the Mexican saddle.

"Oh, Jim! Where did you get that nice saddle?" She touched the silver ornaments that held the saddle strings in place. "This looks like real silver—and look at that beautiful leather tooling!"

"It belonged to Jeremiah Jones, the man who died on the way back from Santa Fe," Jim said. "He must have thought someone would come to Mr. Hood's store to get it, because the last thing he said was to take it to Hood's. Mr. Hood thought I should try it out today to help keep the leather limber. I sure wish it was mine to keep."

Kit nudged Jim's arm. "Don't look now, but someone you know is lookin' at your saddle, and I think he'd like to get it for himself."

Jim felt a sudden sinking in his insides. "Oh, no—not Coy again!"

"Yup—and now he's lookin' at you, and he's got that look on his face. I think he means trouble!"

5

The Goose Pull

Coy was riding a tired-looking gray mule with a saddle that had also seen better days. He did not dismount but walked his mule right up to the rail where Jim had looped Pedro's reins. When his mule held back, reluctant to move into another mule's space, Coy dug his heels into the animal's sides. He forced him so close that Pedro tried to get out of the way.

Jim reached for Pedro's bridle rein. "Easy there," he said, and then to Coy, "Hold your mule back, Colton!"

"Nope. You're in my place. Me and my mule always has this shady spot. *You* get out." He glared at Jim, who was still standing on the other side of Pedro, holding the bridle reins, trying to control his anger.

When Coy noticed the Mexican saddle, he looked back at Jim and said. "That's some fancy saddle for a beanpole like you. How'd you come by it? Seems to me it's a man's saddle, not a baby's."

Jim could only sputter at this new attack. He let go of Pedro's reins and was about to go around the mules to get at Coy when Kit blocked his way and grabbed his arms.

"Hold it, Jim." Kit tightened his grip, and after a moment he felt his friend relax a bit. "You know he's just trying to make you mad."

"Well, he's sure doing it."

Pedro was moving about restlessly, and now he let out a loud bray. Coy tried to hold his animal steady, but the gray mule backed off, almost onto the feet of a man and woman passing by.

Coy paid no attention to the man when he shouted to him to look out, and began moving his mule to force Pedro over again. Kit was still blocking Jim's way.

Martha, blue eyes dark with anger, had been watching from a few feet away. She could take no more. Going around Coy's old mule, which was still trying to back off while Coy tried to force him toward the rail, she cried out, "Coy Colton! You know very well you don't have any special rights to this place! I've had enough of your bullying—you're not going to ruin my afternoon, and I'm not going to let you ruin Jim's. Now get out! Go find another place!"

Coy turned to look at her, speechless for a moment.

A crowd had gathered, and now a couple of the men stepped between Pedro and Coy's mule. One of them was an officer of the club that operated the racetrack.

"Colton," he said, "take your mule and tie it in some open place. Behave yourself, or leave and don't come back."

For once, Coy had nothing to say. He backed his mule from the rail and then turned, heading for a place at the other end.

Martha watched Coy leave. "Good riddance!" she said.

"Nice work, Martha!" Kit said, slapping her on the back.

By this time, Jim had his temper under control. He rubbed Pedro's nose, made sure the reins were secured, and then walked into the racetrack grounds with his friends.

"Thanks, Martha," he said. "If you and Kit hadn't been here, I'd probably have tried to hit him again—and we all know how that would have ended."

The three chose a place to stand near Pedro's hitching rail so that Jim could keep an eye on his animal and the saddle. It was nearly time for the races to start. Jim looked across the open track space to the other side and waved. Mr. and Mrs. Hood were just climbing the bleachers to find a place to sit. Mrs. Hood saw him and returned his wave.

The oval racetrack was a popular place in this frontier town. Some Franklin residents, originally from southern states east of the Mississippi River, had bred and raced fine horses for sport back in the East. Not long after arriving in Franklin, they had formed a club, bought land, and laid out this racetrack. Races and other events were held regularly during the summer and fall.

Now one of the officers of the club came onto the grassy space in the center of the track. He called for those who were racing three-year-old horses to line up at the starting line.

"The fastest horse running fair will win the purse!" he announced, first to the people on one side of the track and then to those on the other.

Four beautiful horses, each with a man of small build in the saddle, lined up. The officer fired a pistol and they were off. The race was once around the track, and dust formed a cloud so thick that the watchers had trouble seeing the finish.

"Sure wish it would rain," Jim said. Inwardly, he thought, *I wish it would rain right away. That would settle the question of the goose pull. Everyone would run for cover and forget the whole thing!*

There were four more races, and though a cloud or two rolled across the sun's face, no rain came to rescue Jim from his predicament.

"Goose pulling is the next event! Open today only to youths under twenty years of age! Riders must be on mules, saddled and bridled!"

After the officer had repeated the announcement for the people on the other side of the track, he called for entrants to go to the starting line.

"Go on, Jim," Kit said. "Take old Pedro and get out there. Mrs. Hood would sure be happy to have a fat goose to cook for dinner. You should try to win it for her."

Jim wasn't so sure. He never had been much good when it came to wringing the necks of chickens or geese back on the farm. He always felt a little sorry for the bird chosen for the family dinner, and he hated to be the one to end its life, especially when it was a loud squawker.

Some of the club men were getting things ready for the contest. One of them came out onto the track with a large gray goose, holding it by the feet, which were tied together. The upside-down bird reached up and tried to bite the man's hand. This didn't seem to bother him, but when the bird bit at his leg, the man struck the bird's head with the side of his hand, and it was quieter.

About halfway up the track, across from the place where Jim, Kit, and Martha were standing, an upright post was attached to the outer rail of the racetrack. It had a brace at the top, supporting a horizontal bar that reached out about three feet over the track. The man with the goose was heading for this post. Another man, mounted on a horse, waited for him.

When the goose was handed up, the man on horseback stood in his stirrups. He secured the goose's feet to the bar, while the man on the ground kept his horse steady. The squawks of the goose were making the animal very uneasy.

"That's why they use mules for the goose pull," Kit said. "My brother William says mules ain't spooked near as easy by loud noises as most horses are."

"Come on, boys!" the announcer called. "Let's have some fun! We need at least four of you out here on mules. Take home a nice fat goose for tomorrow's dinner!"

"Go on, Jim," Martha said. "Look at Mrs. Hood over there, waving to you. She'd like that goose. She could use its feathers for a new pillow, too—maybe she'd give you the pillow!"

"I really don't want to enter," Jim said. "I'll find some other way to get her a goose."

Just then, Coy rode down the track on his mule. He stopped near Jim and stared down at him. Jim could see the hatred in the green eyes, belying his smile and sugary voice. "Why, hello again, Jim Mathews. You have a good mule and a fine saddle. I know that saddle's more'n you're cut out for, but surely you're goin' to come out here and show off!"

"No, thanks." Jim was resolved to hold his temper and ignore Coy's taunts. He looked back to where Pedro stood, sleek and alert. The mule looked right back at him and brayed.

Kit nudged him. "See, Jim—even Pedro wants you to enter. Get in there and snatch that goose right out from under Coy's nose."

Coy heard Kit and smirked. "Oh, we won't make him do it. Daddy's little boy's a-scared he might hurt hisself."

Jim felt his face growing red, but he tightened his lips to keep from saying the words that came to mind.

Coy kicked his mule with his heels and started forward. As he moved away, he spat into the dust at Jim's feet. Martha pulled back in disgust. She turned to Jim. "Are you going to let him do that to you?" she asked.

That settled the matter. To have Martha look down on him was worse than taking part in a contest that he found repulsive. Jim strode across the grass to Pedro, and in a moment he was on the mule's back and riding to the gate. He rode toward the group of entrants. Tom Fuller and two other boys were there, and in a moment Coy joined the group. Jim avoided looking at him.

When the official came with pieces of broomgrass, Jim drew one for his place in the contest. When each of the five boys had drawn a length of straw, the official explained what they were to do. They were to ride one at a time to try to wring the goose's neck, for as many rounds as were necessary. The boy who could actually ride off with the head was the winner. To make it more difficult, bear grease had been rubbed into the bird's neck feathers.

The official read the rules. "The one who has drawn the shortest straw will go first. Next shortest, second—and so on. Fella with the longest straw goes last. He's the lucky one, 'cause you first four fellas will have the goose well loosened by then. Let's see your straws."

Jim's straw was the longest, so he found himself in the number-five position. Coy was number three, and Tom Fuller had drawn the shortest straw.

"Line up," the official called. Then he read the rules loudly so that all in the park could hear them. "Rules are that as soon as the rider crosses the starting line, he puts his mule into a full gallop. He holds him at a gallop, givin' as good a twist as he can to the goose's neck as he goes by, using his right hand only, and not stoppin' or even slowin' the mule. If he hangs on too long, he's likely to fall off the mule, which disqualifies him from the contest."

Then he turned back to the boys. "Good luck to each of you. First rider to the starting line."

Tom, riding a spotted gray mule, went to the line. The official gave his mule a hard slap on the rump to start him off. Tom dug his heels into the mule's sides and galloped up to the goose, reaching for it as he rode by. All he got for his effort was a greasy hand. The goose struggled and honked. Jim's stomach churned at the thought of touching it, but he could not back out now. The second rider had no better luck, and then it was Coy's turn. He gave Jim a sneering look as he rode his mule to the starting line.

Jim's inclination was to scowl back, but instead he found himself smiling and saying, "Do the job, Coy!"

Coy turned quickly. His astonished look made Jim laugh. "Good luck," he called, and meant it. If Coy got the goose, Jim wouldn't even have to touch it.

But Coy wasn't successful either. The goose set up a wild, frantic squawking and flopped about in a great effort to get loose when Coy let go. The head was still firmly attached to the body, although the neck appeared a little stretched out.

The fourth boy felt sure he could take the prize.

"Go to it," Jim said as the boy moved into position. "I hope you get the goose."

"Just watch me," the boy said. "I'll get it, all right!"

But the boy's mule was a bit stubborn. He stopped dead still at the starting line and braced his feet. The rider dug his heels into the animal's sides to get him started, and the official gave the mule an extra-hard slap on the rump.

Laughter came from the crowd. "Hang an apple in front of his nose!" someone called out.

The young man sat bouncing up and down, jabbing his heels into the mule's sides. Even Jim, waiting nervously for his turn, had to laugh.

"Get along there, you stupid beast," the boy said, and gave an extra-hard kick with his heels. Suddenly the mule took off at full speed. The crowd roared with laughter and there was a loud cheer.

The boy got to the goose sooner than he expected. He reached out and gave a hard twist, determined that the laughing should end in a cheer.

Then, "Whoa, whoa!" he yelled. He had hung on too long, and the mule was out from under him. He landed on the dusty track.

He sure does look ridiculous, Jim thought. *I hope to goodness I don't do that!* He patted Pedro, who shifted his weight and snorted as if in reassurance.

The cheering and laughing grew louder. The unfortunate boy sat in the track a moment, scowling. Then, as if part of an act, his mule turned to the crowd and brayed loudly. Grinning now, the young man jumped to his feet, did a little dance step, and gave a deep bow to the audience.

There was a burst of applause. The boy, his face smeared with dust and grease, bowed once more. Automatically out of the contest, he led his now-agreeable mule off toward the gate.

Jim sat on Pedro waiting for things to quiet down. He glanced over to where Martha and Kit stood.

"Stay in there, Jim!" he heard Martha call.

The squawking of the goose had been nearly drowned out by the noise of the crowd, but now both quieted down. The goose hung limp.

I'll be glad when this is over, Jim told himself, *and no more goose pulls for me—ever!*

He braced himself for the ordeal. To be considered a good sport, he would have to make a real try at wringing the bird's neck. The crowd would be quick to boo if they thought he wasn't really trying. The official gave him the signal to start and gave Pedro the usual slap on the rump.

Pedro broke into a gallop, and in almost no time the moment came to reach out for the goose. Jim's right hand closed around the greasy neck feathers and he could feel the struggle of the bird for a moment. The feathers felt warm and slippery. He twisted and tugged at the neck at the moment he was passing by, and held on long enough to be sure it wasn't ready to give. Pedro moved right along as he was supposed to, and Jim let go of the goose in time to keep his seat in the saddle.

As he rode down the track, he could hear the goose squawking, accompanied by light cheering from the crowd.

That's that, he thought as he joined the other three boys still in the contest. They were at the end of the track, ready to head back to the starting line for the second round of tries. Jim turned Pedro, heartily wishing he wouldn't have to touch that warm, greasy neck again. He wiped the grease from his hand onto his pants as he rode along. Mr. Hood's voice could be heard above the others as he passed the crowd. "Get in there, Jim! We're planning on that goose for dinner tomorrow!"

Jim looked over at his employer and smiled the best he could. He waved to Mrs. Hood and rode on. Tom Fuller was ready to start the second round, but there was some delay. The second boy was talking with the official.

"I didn't think it would be like this," he was saying. "I want to drop out."

"Oh, don't do that," the official said. "Let's keep the contest a good one."

"I can't," the boy said. "I feel sick to my stomach."

"What's the matter with mama's boy?" It was Coy. "How 'bout you, Beanpole? You scared too?"

In truth, Jim had been about to tell the official that he wanted to drop out too, but Coy's taunt made him keep silent. Besides, it was highly likely that Coy would get the goose's head off on the second round. The bird had already weakened a great deal. It hung there more quietly now, making a spasmodic movement now and then, its honks just low groans of protest.

Jim turned to Coy, making himself look as fierce as he could. "Just mind you own self, and quit worrying about me. I'll be right behind you to finish off that goose when you fail."

Coy looked a little surprised. "You won't get a chance, Beanpole."

"I hope I don't," Jim muttered under his breath. "I sure don't want to touch it again."

He patted Pedro's neck and lined up behind Coy. Tom Fuller was ready to start.

Then Tom's mule was on its way. The boy had his right arm out, ready to grab the neck. He gave a mighty yank that almost lifted him from his saddle. Feathers flew, but

Tom had to let go and ride on to keep from being pulled off his mount.

For a moment, Jim thought he would disgrace himself by being sick right there in full view of the crowd. When he could look at the goose again, he saw that its neck seemed even longer than before.

Coy moved his mule up to the starting line. From the smile on his face, Jim knew that Coy felt no such pangs of squeamishness. He looked confident.

"Ready, Colton?" asked the official.

"Yeah, I'm ready. And Beanpole here might just as well ride off the track now, 'cause I'm gonna carry away that goose's head."

The official gave Coy's mule a slap, and it broke into a gallop. But then it faltered—Coy was obviously trying to slow the animal down, hoping to give himself more time.

The hanging bird gave a convulsive flop just as Coy's hand grasped its neck. For a moment, the mule almost stopped while Coy gave a mighty wrench. There was another frantic beating of wings and a croaking sound.

Coy was about to separate the head from the rest of the bird when his mule brayed, startled by the bird's beating wings. He jumped, and Coy had to let go. The goose's head hung by a sinew, the neck broken, the skin torn.

The crowd was booing. "No fair! He slowed down! That's cheating!" Only Coy's buddies were cheering.

Jim rode up to the official. "He gets it, doesn't he? It's just hanging by a sinew—and it was Coy who pulled it off."

But the official shook his head. "The goose goes to the one who rides away with the head. Besides, Colton definitely slowed his mule. It was not at a gallop, and Colton had too much time to try."

"I don't want it, sir," Jim said, "Please let Coy have it."

"Now, don't you quit on us. You ride up there and pull that head off properly. The crowd will mob me if I let

Colton have the prize. And that goose isn't dead yet. Its wings are still flopping."

Jim could hardly bear to look. The poor bird was indeed still trying to flap its wings. It looked very feeble, however. He longed just to ride away, but he moved Pedro to the starting line. Looking over at Kit and Martha, he saw that Kit was grinning widely at him, raising his arms as if in a cheer, plainly looking forward to seeing Jim win the prize. Martha smiled, too, and waved at him.

Then he heard Mr. Hood's voice, "Come on, Jim! Goose for dinner tomorrow!"

The thought was almost too much. He swallowed hard and took a deep breath. When his stomach settled down he said, "Let's get it over with. I'm ready."

Then Pedro was galloping up the track. Jim closed his eyes a second and then opened them. It was time to make the grab.

He seized the head and it parted from the body. As Pedro carried him onward, Jim looked down at the ugly, greasy thing in his hand, one round eye open. It was over. Tom Fuller and Coy were already riding back from the end of the track. The official was calling out, "The winner—Jim Mathews! Come on back, Jim, and get your prize!"

Jim looked back. With the help of another man, the official was getting the goose down from the rack. But Jim could take no more. He looked again at the goose head and threw it to the gound. "Let Coy or Tom have it!" he yelled, and turned Pedro toward the gateway. Pedro seemed to know what his rider wanted. He left the racetrack at a gallop, hiding Jim in a cloud of dust as they went out to the road.

Mule and rider headed westward, away from the crowd. But suddenly Jim knew he had to stop Pedro and dismount. He pulled at the reins, and the mule stopped willingly in the shade of a tree.

With the tree to shield him from the eyes of anyone who might have watched, Jim let go and was sick.

He was standing there a few minutes later, his right hand on the pommel of the beautiful saddle, his forehead against Pedro's neck, when he heard Martha's voice.

"Are you all right?"

Jim made himself face her. "Of course, Martha. I was just going to come back."

Martha laid her hand on his arm. "You don't have to explain. I guess I know how you feel. But Mr. Hood is very proud of you."

"Did they give the goose to Coy?"

"No. They said that Coy broke the rules. Mr. Hood accepted the goose for you."

Jim could smile now, weakly. "Martha, may I have dinner with your family tomorrow? If you aren't having goose, that is. . . ."

Martha laughed. "Mama will be happy to have company for Sunday dinner. And we are not having goose!"

6

Trouble at the Warehouse

JIM was out sweeping the wooden walkway in front of the store early Monday morning when Kit's brother Robert rode up. Robert was a muscular young man of twenty-two who had been following the Santa Fe Trail for several years.

"Mornin', Jim. I heard you didn't enjoy the goose."

Jim grinned. "Guess you heard right."

"Kit asked me to tell you he'll be around lookin' for you after work tonight. He's been tryin' to talk Ma into lettin' him quit his 'prenticeship and go along on the next caravan."

"I know. He told me he wants to go somethin' awful."

"Kit thinks you should go along, too, and try to find your pa out there."

"I sure would like to—maybe I will. But Pa did tell me to wait here until he got back. I keep hopin' someone will bring word from him and then I'll know what to do."

Robert dismounted and slung the bridle reins around the hitching rail in front of the store. "Well, Jim, with Jeremiah Jones gone, I think word from your pa out in those mountains is likely gone too. You just might have to decide on your own. Think you're man enough to do that?"

Jim leaned on the broom, a puzzled frown on his face. Robert paused before going into the store, waiting for an answer.

"Guess I am," Jim told him. "I didn't back off from Coy Colton the other night."

Robert started into the store, paused, and then came back. "Jim, sometimes bein' a man means usin' good judgment 'stead of flyin' out with your fists. There's more to bein' a man—or a woman, for that matter. It means a lot of things—like puttin' other people ahead of yourself when you're tryin' to decide somethin', for one. And livin' up to what you know is right."

Jim didn't know what to say. Robert saved him the trouble by changing the subject. "Well, I've got to see if Hood has some good bolts of cloth left. We want to take some on the next caravan. William, Ham, and me are goin' back for the last trip before winter sets in. We'll be leavin' in less'n two weeks, Jim. Better be thinkin' over what I told you before you decide if you're goin' out lookin' for your pa. Personally, I think you're bitin' off more'n you can chew." He went on into the store.

The boy leaned on the broom for a moment longer before he went back to the sweeping. He would love to go with that caravan, but Robert's words troubled him. He'd have to do a lot of thinking in the next few days. If only Pa had come back, or at least sent him a letter . . .

The day was hot and muggy, threatening rain but not bringing any relief from the heat. By noon, Jim's shirt was soaked with sweat, for Mr. Hood had put him to work stacking merchandise onto the empty spaces on the shelves. Earlier, the two of them had brought a wagon-load of goods from the warehouse down on the river-front. The warehouse had been built close to the river so that goods could be unloaded from the boats and stored with as little hauling as possible.

Jim ate his noon meal in the backyard under the sycamore tree. Mrs. Hood was serving cold sliced goose to her husband, but she fixed Jim a plate of beans, potatoes, and ham.

"Jim, you know how much I appreciate your getting that goose for me," she had said when she brought him his food. "But I can also understand why you suddenly don't like goose meat." She smiled at him warmly before she left.

The store was closed for the noon hour, and Mr. Hood had given Jim his instructions for the afternoon before he went to the house. Jim was to walk back to the warehouse when he finished eating. Going there was lots more interesting than working in the store, for he could take time to look at the boats tied at the wharf. There were keelboats, flatboats, and even an occasional steamboat there. The boatmen talked of things they had seen and done in faraway places. They had all been to St. Louis, and some even to New Orleans. A few had been up the Missouri, too—all places that Jim dreamed of going to someday.

In the warehouse, he was to count the bolts of cloth that were still there, left from the big shipment purchased in Philadelphia, Pennsylvania, last spring. The cloth had been taken from there to Pittsburgh by freight wagon, and then by steamboat down the Ohio River, up the Mississippi to St. Louis, and then up the Missouri River to Franklin. Even though the cloth had to be priced high to pay for all the transportation costs, it still brought a profit when sold in Santa Fe.

"Then check the barrels," Mr. Hood had said. "Write down what's in the full ones, and how many usable empties there are. When you finish, go over to the cooper's and ask him if he can make me some more barrels before the first of November. We'll buy as much pork on the hoof as we can take care of, Jim, but we'll need to get more barrels and salt to pack the meat for shipping. You and I'll be plenty busy right up to when the river freezes. We'll get our shipments off to Fort Atkinson up at Council Bluffs first, and those to the New Orleans market after it's too cold to start boats upriver."

Mr. Hood was certainly planning on having him as a helper all winter. "Yes, sir," Jim had said, "but—" then he stopped. Maybe he'd better not say anything about going with the caravan to find Pa. Not yet, anyway.

"But what, Jim?"

"Nothing, sir. I'll get along down to the warehouse as soon as I finish my dinner."

Mr. Hood had taken the warehouse key from its hook on the store wall. "Put the key in your pocket now, so you won't go off without it. And be sure to lock up when you're through down there." He started to walk away. Then he turned back and said, "Oh—one more thing, Jim. While you're on the riverfront, please go to the ropewalk and tell Bernard I'm going to need a lot more rope for the next caravan. Ask him if he'll take some good hemp one of the farmers left with me in payment."

"Yes, sir. Guess I'll be gone most of the afternoon, don't you think?"

"You just might. I won't look for you back here until about sundown." From the smile on Mr. Hood's face, Jim knew it was all right to spend some time looking at the boats and watching the boatmen at work.

As he walked toward the river, Jim went over his assignments, hoping not to forget anything. Soon he could see the warehouse—a long log building with a small door on one end and a big one on the side facing the river. There'd been a bad flood there last spring, but luckily Mr. Hood had had all his goods moved out in time. Now the weather was so dry and the river so low that it seemed impossible the water could ever have been standing three feet deep in the building. Another man's warehouse had collapsed in the flood, and some of the ground in front of

Mr. Hood's property had washed into the river. If any more of the riverbank went, Mr. Hood's warehouse would go with it. Franklin businessmen worried about the floods every spring, and some had even moved their warehouses away to higher ground.

Jim had the key to the small door. The other door was barred from the inside. The key went into the rusty lock easily, since he and Mr. Hood had been there just that morning, but the door creaked loudly on its leather hinges as it always did. A rat scurried away as daylight fell upon it. Jim hadn't felt at all scared here in the morning with Mr. Hood, but now he shivered a little.

Waiting a moment, he let his eyes adjust to the dimness in the warehouse. There were no windows in the big room. A few narrow beams of sunlight cut through the dusty air from cracks between the logs of the wall and between the top of the wall and the roof, above the stacked boxes and barrels. To give himself more light, Jim left the door wide open behind him as he went inside.

Off to the right were the boxes that held cloth for the Santa Fe trade. These boxes contained some of the finest materials from New England and other parts of the world. Mr. Hood had the cloth well wrapped and boxed to protect it from mice and insects that might otherwise feed upon it.

Wish I'd brought a lantern, Jim said to himself. It was hard to read the markings on the boxes, and he was supposed to check the number of bolts of cloth stored in each. It took a long time to count them and make his notes on a scrap of paper.

"Fifteen bolts of cotton goods, five of wool, ten of linen, one of silk—that seems to be all the cloth," he said aloud, reading over his list. His voice sounded strange in the silence of the building. *I'll be glad to get out of here,* he thought. He was ready to go over to Mr. Bernard's and see about the rope.

As he left the warehouse, he locked the door behind him. It felt good to be out in the open air, even though it was so hot.

The ropewalk was a long one-story building where rope was made from hemp fibers. The settlers near Franklin grew the hemp on the low, damp fields along the river. Jim entered through a door at one end and walked past piles of gray fiber and coils of finished rope. Off to the left was a complicated arrangement of wheels and pulleys used to twist the fibers into rope. Workers walked back and forth, guiding the lengthy twists of hemp.

Mr. Bernard was seated high on a stool at a tall desk near the far end of the building, writing in his record book. He looked up and greeted Jim as the boy came near.

"Hello there, Jim. Hot day, isn't it? Doesn't seem likely to rain, either. Sure would feel good to get a good soaking." He laid down his quill pen and wiped the perspiration from his face and bald head with a red bandanna.

Jim agreed and said, "Mr. Hood sent me to ask if you have enough rope on hand to give him more. He's looking to outfit the next Santa Fe caravan. And he wants to know if you will take hemp in trade."

Mr. Bernard wiped his hands with the bandanna and then nodded. "Tell him we can use all the hemp we can get. We have orders from St. Louis for more rope than we can make."

"Thank you," Jim said. "I'll tell him." He decided to leave by the door near Mr. Bernard's desk instead of the one through which he had entered. This would give him a longer walk along the riverfront and a chance to look over the boats that were there. Keelboats were tied at both docks, taking on loads. At the ferryboat landing, a man was guiding his wagon and team on board the ferry that would take them across the river to Boonville.

Someday I'm going to cross this river, Jim thought. He tried to picture what it would be like to leave Franklin, the only place he could remember except for the farm and nearby Fort Kincaid. If he went with the caravan, the river crossing would be a little farther to the northwest, at Arrow Rock.

He sat on a log to watch the riverfront activity awhile, and his mind drifted to thoughts of Santa Fe. *It won't be too hard to find out where Pa is camped if I go there,* he reasoned, not knowing the actual difficulties of travel in mountain country with winter coming on. He figured he'd go on up to Taos where he'd find Mr. Ewing Young, who would tell him where to find his pa. His thoughts created an imaginary beaver camp, far from the Franklin riverfront, and he didn't notice the arrival of a wagon alongside one of the docks. Then an all-too-familiar voice reached his ears.

"Whoa, *whoa!* Stand still, you dumb mules!"

Coy Colton again. Jim couldn't seem to get away from him. He watched as Coy jumped down from the wagon seat and started toward one of the keelboats. Even the sight of him brought a sinking feeling to Jim's insides and a buzzing to his head.

The boatman in charge called out to Coy, "Be ready to load that flour in about ten minutes. Just leave your wagon there until we have this other stuff moved into the cargo box."

Jim tried to walk away from the docks without being seen by Coy. He still had to go to the cooper's—and he suddenly remembered that he hadn't counted the barrels in the warehouse. He'd better get on with his work. Hurrying now, he left his message at the cooper's and headed back to the warehouse.

There was even less light in the building than before— the sun was getting lower—and again he left the door open for light.

The empty barrels had not been separated from the full ones, and Jim had to tap on them to decide which was which. He counted twenty new barrels, usable for packing pork. Some of the old barrels could be used too, but he had to look them over for soundness. He climbed up onto a barrel, and from its smell he knew it contained vinegar. Planks were laid across the upright sealed barrels to give support to the barrels on top. Jim stepped from the front to the rows behind the first. The barrels were stacked two high.

"Seems to me that we put quite a few empty barrels on top," Jim said, breaking the stillness of the room. "But I thought there were some full of whiskey and wine that we hoisted up here too."

He knocked on the side of a barrel.

Full, he decided from the sound. Behind it, he knocked and found one that was empty. He wanted to test more of the barrels, but it was too dark, and some were packed too closely to be reached.

He decided to roll a few of the empties out of the way to get back to the last row. He took hold of the one nearest him, turning it on its rim until he could get behind it. There was a scurrying sound, and he stepped back quickly.

"Doggone rats," he said aloud. He hesitated before moving into the space he had made.

Suddenly there was a new sound. Someone was behind him on the plank from which he had stepped. He turned quickly.

Coy stood there, not an arm's length away. Instinctively, Jim reached out to hold him off, but Coy's big hand closed around Jim's wrist.

"I've got you this time, Beanpole," Coy said. "An' this time I'll learn you to keep that skinny fist in your pocket when you're around me." He gave a sharp twist to Jim's arm, and Jim bit his lip to keep from crying out.

"Come on! Tell me what you think of that!" Coy twisted more. It was all Jim could do to keep from screaming, but instead he said, "I'll stay out of your way, Coy."

Coy relaxed his grip a little and the pain eased, but he didn't let go. "That's better, Beanpole. But I wanna be sure you remember it." With this, he flipped Jim, throwing him down onto the barrel tops. The barrel rims were like knives cutting into his back.

"That's just the beginnin'," he said. "That's just for the little mean thing you did in takin' that goose when you knew I had wrung its neck."

Jim tried to get up, only to find Coy's foot on his chest. "I told them to give it to you, Coy."

"Yeah? You expect me to believe that? Then how come they didn't give it to me?"

" 'Cause they said you broke the rules. You slowed your mule."

Suddenly Jim was on his feet again—pulled up by Coy.

"You liar!" Coy shouted into his face. "You dirty liar! Now I'm really gonna give it to you! For that and for pokin' me in the nose Friday night!"

Jim was helpless as Coy swung him around. He was thrown to the dirt floor of the warehouse and thought he would never breathe again. Coy jumped down and stood over him.

"And this is for snickerin' at me when we was kids back in school!"

So that was what Coy had against him all these years!

"I wasn't making fun of you—" he started to say, and tried to get up.

But he was knocked back down with a slam. He felt the thrust of a knee against his ribs and a fist in his left eye. It was the last thing he remembered.

7

Kit's Secret

JIM thought he heard his father calling. "Oh, Jim . . . Jim-boy! What happened to you?" The voice was pleasantly familiar, but it wasn't his pa calling him Jim-boy. It was Mr. Hood.

Pain came back, and with it the memory of where he was and why he hurt so much. He tried to open his eyes, but they seemed glued shut.

"Jim-boy! Can you hear me?"

"Mmmm . . ." It was more a groan than a reply. Aware now of the pain and swelling in his left eye, he forced himself to open his right one. He saw the rays of light from a lantern, and then Mr. Hood bending over him.

"Good heavens! What happened to you, boy? Who gave you such a beating?"

"Coy—he got even with me."

"I'd say he more than got even, Jim. Let's see if you can sit up. Wait—let me help you."

He set the lantern down and put his arm under Jim's shoulders. Knowing he must, Jim allowed Mr. Hood to raise him to a sitting position. He thought he had never felt so terrible in all his life and leaned forward, resting his head in his hands.

"I'm sorry," he mumbled. Mr. Hood leaned over Jim, waiting for the boy to steady himself. After a moment, Jim looked up and said, "I forgot to count the empty barrels when I stopped here the first time. I came in again, and Coy followed me up from the dock. He was down there with a load of flour. I—I didn't hear him come in."

"Let's see if you can stand up and walk. We should try to start for home—it's quite dark outside."

On his feet, Jim had to hold onto Mr. Hood to fight the dizziness, but after a moment he felt a bit steadier. "I think I can walk now," he said.

Mr. Hood picked up the lantern as they went out the door. Slowly, they made their way up the dirt street, Mr. Hood supporting Jim and holding the lantern to light the way. Jim's head felt better, but he was sore all over, especially around his ribs and where his back had hit the barrel rims. Every step was painful, and it seemed to take hours to reach the store.

Kit was waiting there.

"What in the world happened to you?" He stared at Jim, who was limping and had a swollen eye turned purple as grape juice.

"Tangled with Coy, and he came out on top," Jim said.

Mr. Hood helped him through the store, with Kit following. "Let's get that shirt off and fix you up," Mr. Hood said when they reached the storeroom. "I need your help, Kit. Get me a basin of water."

Kit filled Jim's washbasin and brought it into the storeroom. Mr. Hood had set his lantern on the box Jim used for a table, and now he set to work washing Jim's wounds. He sent Kit to the house for some of Mrs. Hood's salve and eyewash.

"Ask her to bring something for Jim to eat, too."

An hour later, Jim was feeling much better. Mrs. Hood's soothing salve and eyewash were doing their work. He had on his clean blue shirt and had eaten warm buttered johnny-cake and a large helping of pork and beans. He and Kit went out to sit on the edge of the raised walkway in front of the store. Kit seemed unusually quiet.

"What's the matter?" Jim asked. "Did you get in some kind of trouble with Mr. Workman?"

"No." Kit kicked at a lump of dirt, and Jim waited for him to go on. "Robert came by this afternoon. He says that I can't go on the caravan this year—or maybe even next. William and him talked things over, and they decided they wouldn't go against Ma.

"What did your ma say?"

"That my stepfather and her don't want me to quit my 'prenticeship. My brothers won't let me go with them, not unless Ma changes her mind." Kit got to his feet and kicked again, raising the dust. Then he leaned over the hitching rail, his back to Jim.

"I don't know what to do," he said. He straightened up and then suddenly struck the rail with his fist. "I can't stay here and make harnesses for city folk another whole year!"

"If you stay, I'll stay."

Kit turned to face his friend. "Jim, you forget I'm a lot older'n you. I'll be seventeen years old this Christmas! I may be short and look like a kid, but I'm old enough to do a man's work. And I don't want that work to be makin' harness for fancy carriages!"

"I feel like I'm old enough to take care of myself, too, Kit. I'm nearly fifteen and a half."

Kit looked at Jim's swollen eye, now an even deeper purple, and his bright blue eyes twinkled. "I think some folks might argue 'bout your bein' able to take care o' yourself, Jim. Have you looked in a mirror lately?"

Jim reached up and touched his left eye gingerly. "That's just 'cause I tangled with Coy. But he ought to be satisfied now. He was still mad about Friday night and even madder that he didn't get that ol' goose. Called me a liar when I said I asked them to give it to him."

"Look, Jim—he'll keep findin' things to be mad about. You'd better get out of his way and come with me to Santa Fe."

Jim looked sharply at Kit. "I thought you just said you couldn't go to Santa Fe—"

Kit turned away. "Well, I can't get permission to go." Then he faced Jim. "But there's other ways. Look, I'm almost as old now as my brother Ham was when he went for the first time. Him and Robert both told Ma it would be all right for me to go, but it's my stepfather who's so set on me learnin' a trade. He says I should stay with the Workman brothers till I finish my 'prenticeship. And Ma does what he says, so she said no."

"Then what do you mean about my going with you?"

Kit rubbed one foot back and forth in the dust before he answered. "Can you keep a secret?"

"Sure—cross my heart."

"Well, I've got it all figured out. When the caravan leaves next week, I'll say good-bye to my brothers and go back to the Workmans'. But after dark, I'll take off and catch up with the caravan. If I stay out of sight for a couple of days, they won't have the heart to make me go back."

"Won't Mr. Workman try to find you?"

Kit shrugged his shoulders. "Maybe. But if I travel at night and hide in the daytime, I should be safe."

"What will you eat?"

"I'll pack some bread and stuff before I go. And when I'm far enough away, I can shoot squirrels. I've got a good rifle and a saddle, and that's about all a man needs to get along."

Jim sighed. "Sounds exciting, Kit. But I'll miss you somethin' awful."

"Well, why don't you come along?"

Jim was silent, thinking the matter over. He started to lean back on his elbows, but his ribs hurt and he straightened up again. "I don't know," he said. "Maybe I will. I couldn't get in much more trouble than I do around here. And I'll find my pa out there."

"That's right. My brothers know how to find David Kincaid, and he could tell you about your pa."

The sound of hooves and wagon wheels interrupted their talk.

"Sounds like they're comin' from the east," Kit said. "Likely to join the caravan. Let's go down to the corner and see who it is."

Jim eased himself up and followed slowly. They watched a party of travelers come in on the old Boonslick Trail from St. Charles, Missouri, northwest of St. Louis.

The group was led by a pair of riders. As they drew near, the boys could see that one was a young man and the other a boy. Both were slight of build, with dark hair showing from under the broad-brimmed hats worn by most westbound travelers. Each sat his horse with his back straight and his shoulders back.

"Hey, I know that man!" Kit cried. "That's Charles Bent from St. Louis. He worked with my brother Moses in the Missouri Fur Company and came to our cabin to visit one time. He's a real important man in the fur trade."

Behind the two dark-haired riders were other men mounted on horses and mules, and a big freight wagon covered with canvas stretched over hoops. The group stopped as they came onto the square.

Kit ran over to where the two lead riders had stopped. Jim followed more slowly.

"Hello, Mr. Bent!" Kit called. "I'm Moses Carson's brother Kit. Remember me?"

Charles Bent looked down at the stocky boy standing in the road. "Why, certainly I remember you, Kit. How's the littlest Carson?"

Kit grinned. "I guess I am the runt of the family, Mr. Bent. Goin' to be around awhile?"

The man nodded. "Yes, until the caravan gets under-way. I'd like you to meet my brother William. He's just about your age." He turned to the boy waiting quietly on his horse. "Will, here's someone for you to get to know while we're here in Franklin. This is Kit Carson. If Kit's like the other Carson boys, it won't be long before he's going west too."

Will Bent smiled, white teeth showing in his dark face. "Glad to meet you, Kit."

Kit turned to Jim, who was standing behind him. "This is my friend, Jim Mathews. Don't mind his looks—he got into a bad fight today."

It hurt to smile, but Jim did the best he could. He shook hands, first with Charles Bent and then with young Will. Will was a carbon copy of his older brother, but his size was that of the average twelve- or thirteen-year-old boy.

"Well, we'll be seeing you boys," Charles Bent said. "We're heading over to McNees' place to put up while we're in town. Good night now."

He walked his horse back to point out their destination to the wagon driver, and then the whole group moved on to the west side of the square, where McNee's Union Hall stood. The Union Hall was an inn with a large fenced yard where wagons could be kept, and a stable for horses and mules.

Kit and Jim walked back to the store and sat down again. Kit's eyes shone eagerly in the light that came from the store's lamps.

"Did you see that Will Bent, how little he is? Jim, he's not as tall as me, and much skinnier. But his older brother wants him along, little as he is."

"He sure is a little guy, all right. But I'll bet he's as old as you, Kit, or even older. He looked like he was pretty grown-up, except in size."

"But if he can go west, so can I! My mind's made up, Jim. I'm goin'."

Kit got up and paced back and forth. Then he said, "Jim, why don't you start plannin' too?"

Jim ran his fingers through his dark hair. He started to say something and then stopped, looking down at the weeds growing along the edge of the walkway.

"Come on, Jim—say you'll go too."

"I'd sure like to," Jim said after a pause. "But I don't quite know what to do. If only Pa'd sent some kind of word—"

"Maybe he told Jones to tell you to come out on the next caravan and he'd meet you at Santa Fe."

"Yeah, and maybe he didn't. And another thing, Kit— Mr. Hood is making all sorts of plans for me to help him this fall and winter."

"I think you should go, same as me. Anyway, you think about it. I gotta go back to Workmans' now." He turned to leave and then came back. "Swear you won't tell my secret."

Jim stood up and marked out a cross with his finger over his chest. "Cross my heart and hope to die."

Kit seemed satisfied. "See you tomorrow—and stay out of trouble!"

Mr. Hood came to the door. "I'm locking up, Jim. Better get yourself to bed."

"Yes, sir. I'll come around to the back in just a couple of minutes."

The lights of the store went out, but Jim sat a little longer. It was quiet in the square. There wasn't even much noise from McNees'. The Bent party had settled in for the night, Jim supposed. The Square and Compass was quiet too.

"Guess I'd better turn in, even if I am too sore to sleep," Jim said aloud. He walked around the side of the store to his place at the back. Moonlight brightened the street somewhat, but the way beside the store was dark.

About halfway to the back of the building, someone coming from the Hood's yard brushed past him.

"Hey, what are you doing here?" Jim demanded.

But whoever it was ran on. Jim followed to the front of the building and was just in time to see a dark shape cross the road, bare feet thudding as he went. The figure was definitely not that of Coy Colton—it was much smaller.

Some little kid out later'n he ought to be, Jim thought. *Likely he was too scared to answer.*

He turned and went back around the store. Everything looked normal. The storeroom door was open, as Mr. Hood had left it. Jim went inside and pulled the lower half of the door closed.

Air's so hot, I'll leave the top half open, he thought. *This is one night I won't have to worry about Coy.* He didn't bother with lighting his candle. His muscles and bruises ached, so he decided to put some more of Mrs. Hood's salve on the worst places. A breeze came up as he finished, and the air felt cooler. *Now I think I might be able to go to sleep,* he thought, and stretched out on his bed. As he lowered his head, he felt something on the pillow.

"What in the world—?" Jim sat up again and picked up a piece of paper. He could see words scrawled on it in large letters. He took it to the open door, where the moonlight was bright enough for him to read the crude writing.

GIT OUT oᴺ TOWN

Jim felt that sinking feeling again. That kid in the alley must have been Coy's messenger.

Maybe he should "git out of town." Maybe he should take this as a sign and go west with Kit. Then he realized that Kit's secret had suddenly become his secret too.

8

A Surprise for Jim

JIM spent an uneasy night and felt tired and worried the next morning. While on his way to the Franklin Post Office to pick up Mr. Hood's mail, an idea came to him. Perhaps someone had left a message for him at the post office!

Mr. Hood's letters in hand, Jim spoke to the postmaster. "I don't suppose anyone brought in a letter or some kind of message for me, Mr. Samuel. . . ."

Mr. Samuel peered at Jim over his small glasses. "You wouldn't be looking for some word from your father, would you, boy?"

"Yes, sir."

Mr. Samuel shuffled through some letters in the M pigeonhole. "Nothing here for Mathews. Haven't you heard from your pa since he left, Jim?"

"No, sir. Seems he's stayed out there to trap beaver. It's likely he asked Jeremiah Jones to get word to me, but Jones got killed out at the Cimarron."

Mr. Samuel shook his head. "I know—I heard. Too bad, too bad. Well, your pa will come back soon, and he'll be right proud to see what a fine fellow you've grown into. That is, if you keep out of the way of big bullies like that Colton fellow!" Mr. Samuel's eyes twinkled through his steady gaze.

Jim became conscious of his appearance, and he grinned sheepishly. "Guess you're right, Mr. Samuel. I'm gonna try, anyway."

As he walked back toward the store, Jim felt discouraged. It was bad enough that news of Coy's thrashing was all over town—now he felt as if everyone knew about his pa, too, and pitied him. *Pa should have put somethin' in writin', 'stead of countin' on Jones to tell me what he was doin'.* Resentment and anger at his pa came back, and again he remembered the time after his mother died. Had his pa walked out on him again—this time never to return?

His ribs and back hurt him, and his head ached again. None of this would have happened if his pa had been there like he promised. He'd never have got into this mess with Coy—it was all his pa's fault!

"Morning, Jim. You look like you lost your last friend." It was Martha, on her way to the post office.

Jim looked up, and Martha saw his bruised face.

"Oh, for goodness sake! You look awful! What did you do to yourself?"

"I didn't do it to myself. Coy came lookin' for me down at the warehouse and beat me up."

Martha reached out with her forefinger and gently touched the bruised eye. "Does it hurt as bad as it looks? Maybe Daddy could help." Her voice was softer now.

"It'll be all right in a couple of days. I won't need to bother the doctor with it." He smiled. "Every guy gets a black eye once in a while."

"Until he grows up!" Martha's voice was no longer gentle, but she smiled a bit. "You seem to think hitting will settle matters—these last few days you're getting into more than your share of trouble, Jim."

"Yeah, I know. It's 'cause of my pa—if only he'd kept his promise and come back with the others, everything would be fine and I wouldn't be all banged up."

"You can't blame it all on your father!" Martha shook her head. "He didn't make you lose your temper—and that's really what started all this. You did it to yourself."

Jim avoided Martha's gaze. When she spoke again, she spoke as a friend. "You know he cares about you, Jim. After all, you're the most important person in the world to him. Don't go blaming him until you learn the truth."

Jim looked down at the street and said nothing as he tried to think of what to say. When he finally raised his head, he was smiling. "I guess you're right. I'll remember what you said."

"Promise?"

"Promise. I got to get back to the store now. See you later."

They parted, and Jim hurried into the square. Horses were tied at the hitching rail outside the store. *Customers,* he thought, *and I should be helping.* As he went inside, he recognized Charles and Will Bent.

"You wouldn't believe the number of beaver in the streams, Robert," Charles was saying. "Enough to make a man rich in just a few seasons. And it would be a big mistake for a fur company like ours not to set up a trading post. We've got to get right to the source of the furs."

Will turned when he heard Jim enter. "Aren't you the one who was with Kit Carson last night when we came into town?" Will asked. He held out his hand and smiled.

Jim stepped forward to shake hands. Will's grip was strong, and Jim noticed how muscular he was. *Small, yes,* he told himself, *but powerfully built.*

"Yes. I'm Jim Mathews. I work for Mr. Hood."

"Jim," Mr. Hood said, "this is Mr. Charles Bent. He's an officer in Pilcher and Company, the new fur-trading company that's looking to get in on the fur trade out where your pa is. They're considering buildin' a trading post out there."

Charles, too, offered his hand, and he smiled just as his brother had. With their hats removed, the brothers looked alike, each with a full head of thick black hair. Their skin was tanned and weathered from spending much time outdoors.

Charles turned back to the business of stocking up for the caravan. Jim and Will fell into conversation.

"I heard you and your brother are headin' west in a few days. Will this be your first trip with the caravan?"

"Oh, no," Will responded. "I went up the Missouri to work for his fur company last year."

"Didn't your folks object? You can't be much older than I am."

Will's white teeth flashed again. "I'm older than you might think. I was seventeen last May. That's old enough. Charles went west when he was about my age, and he didn't have any older brother to look after him."

"Is your father in the fur business too?"

"No. My father is a judge in St. Louis—Judge Bent. He used to work for the United States Government."

"Doesn't he want you to stay in St. Louis and learn a trade?"

Will smiled. "Well, I guess so. But he understands how it is to want to see new parts of the world. When he was young, he went from Virginia 'cross the mountains to Ohio. Then he went to St. Louis before Lewis and Clark had finished exploring the Louisiana Territory. He made me stay home till I was sixteen, but he knows how it is to want to go out into the wilderness."

Jim nodded. He was hoping he might learn something to help Kit—perhaps even himself. "I suppose you learned a lot from your brother, even before you went up the Missouri last year."

"Yes, but not nearly as much as I learned just by goin'. One thing I learned is that it sure helps to know how to get along with Indians, and how to speak a little of their languages. That's real important if you're goin' west."

"I know a few words from Indians that live around here," Jim said. "The ones that are still here get along with the settlers, but when we came here from Kentucky, there were several attacks. We had to stay in the forts quite often. That's where Kit and I got to be friends. His family was staying in the same fort—Kincaid's fort."

There was silence for a moment. Then Jim plunged into asking about what he really wanted to know. "Hey, Will—let's say a boy like me or Kit wanted to go along on the caravan, but we didn't have money to buy our provisions or anything. Is there a job a boy could get? One that would earn his keep along the trail?"

"Well, yes, sometimes. Sometimes a man has more animals than he can handle alone and needs a boy that's good with mules or horses to help him." Will looked sharply at Jim. "Are you and Kit goin' on the caravan?"

Jim had to be careful not to give away Kit's secret. He lowered his voice. "Well, we haven't really decided. We both want to go, but Kit's supposed to stay here and work out another year of his 'prenticeship. And his step-father said he couldn't go."

"Three of his brothers are going, aren't they? Won't they let him go with them?"

"His brothers would let him, but his mother says no. Maybe it's 'cause Kit was always so small and she's worried that somethin' might happen to him."

"My mother didn't want me to go," Will said, " 'specially after our baby brother died two years ago. Mothers are that way. But how about you—are your folks goin' to let you go?"

Jim explained about his mother's death and his father's absence. He finished by saying, "Sure thought I'd be goin' trappin' with Pa this winter, but I guess he decided he'd rather start without me."

"Well, if this was his first trip west, I know a little about what your father learned on the trail. It's a rough life, and even rougher goin' off into the mountains to trap. Maybe he thought you oughta grow more before he risked your life. You're still pretty young, you know."

"But all he had to do was send word—I'd have understood. I wouldn't mind waitin' if I knew that he hadn't forgot about me."

Will saw that Jim wasn't far from tears. "Hey—he wouldn't forget you. Just wait and see. You'll find out sooner or later." Will talked as if he were Jim's older brother. He held out his hand. "If you're goin' to be a trapper, we're bound to meet again, Jim. Let's shake on it!"

Jim felt better as he and Will turned back to the men. "If my plans to build a fort in the Colorado River basin work out," Charles Bent was saying, "I'll be sending back for more supplies as soon as the weather permits. The way Astor's men have cut into the northern trade, I've got to look to the southern Rockies for good business."

"The men tell me it's dry as a bone along some stretches of the trail," Mr. Hood said. "Are you prepared for that?"

"I only mean to follow the Santa Fe as far as the Cimarron crossin'. We're gonna leave the caravan there and head on ourselves along the Arkansas River. We'll find out if wagons can go that way, and if they can, I'm sure a trading post would do good business out there."

Mr. Hood agreed. "Five years ago, no one would've thought that the Santa Fe trade would build up like it has. An experienced man like you should be able to make it. That is, if you're lucky and don't meet an Indian war party."

"Can't blame 'em for tryin' to stop the white man from takin' their hunting lands," Bent said. "I expect to do good business with the Indians as well as with white trappers—or black or any color of skin, for that matter. If I get my fort built, I'll apply for appointment as Indian agent and see if I can't work things out peaceably."

He turned to the two boys. "I'm going to need you two in a minute," he said. "Mr. Hood tells me you're a good hand with mules, Jim."

Jim felt sharp eyes looking him over and suddenly became conscious of his too-short trousers. He felt the blood rushing to his cheeks under that studying look and knew he must be blushing.

"Jim's a better judge of mules than I am," Mr. Hood said. Charles smiled and put an arm on Jim's shoulders. His eyes were level with the boy's.

"Come on, then. Let's go pick out some mules. I need a coupla good teams to pull the wagons I'm buyin'."

Feeling important, Jim led the way out of the store. A minute later he was seated behind Will on the younger Bent's horse. He told Charles the route to Mr. Hood's pasture lot and they started out.

There was something about being this close to the Bent brothers that made Jim feel he was part of their life in the West. He had a glimpse of what it would be like to spend the winter trading with Indians out there, looking for a place to build a fort in the wilderness. Being with them and hearing of their experiences was exciting for a boy who had seen so little of the world.

The excitement lasted into the next week as Jim worked with the Bent brothers at the pasture, putting in two hours a day to help with training the teams they bought. Time passed quickly, and there was little left for thinking of his personal problems.

At the store, Mr. Hood had much for Jim to do. Most days he couldn't even leave to help Martha with the water bucket. There was extra business from those who were preparing for the westward journey. Jim was kept busy packing boxes and wrapping bales of goods to be taken to Santa Fe. The caravan would leave in the middle of September, and the first week of the month was already gone.

On the last day of working with the mules, Jim and Will went to the pasture without Charles. Jim was riding behind Will as usual when he saw the flour-mill wagon coming toward them. Coy Colton was driving the team.

"Will," Jim said, "that guy coming this way is the one who beat me up just before you came to Franklin."

"The one who gave you that shiner?"

"He's the one. His name is Coy Colton."

"Should I spook his team to get even?"

"No." Jim laughed, and then added, "But when he sees me, he might try some trick. Keep an eye on him."

"Keep your head down and maybe he won't notice you."

But Jim was taller than Will, and there was little he could do to hide. He knew the instant he was recognized, for Coy started heading his team over to crowd Will's horse off the road.

"I told you he's mean," Jim muttered.

"We'll show him up a bit. Hold on real tight."

The wagon was coming closer and Will's horse had scarcely enough room to stay on the roadway.

"Here goes!" Will said. Suddenly he let out a shrill scream—a Comanche yell, he said later—and urged his horse forward. Coy pulled on the reins as his team shied, and the roadway opened for Will and Jim.

As they passed on Will's galloping horse, Jim heard Coy shout, "I'll get you for this, Mathews!"

When Will had slowed the horse to a walk once more, Jim looked back. The wagon was hidden in a cloud of dust.

"I'll probably have night visitors again," he said, and he told Will about the night Coy had tried to break in.

Will laughed. "I can just see that big galoot sprawled out. Served him right!"

"Yeah, but he doesn't forget. You saw how I looked after he beat me up at the warehouse. Then he had a kid leave a note in my room telling me to get out of town. This is the first time I've seen him since then."

They arrived at the pasture gate, and Jim slid down to open it. After the horse went through, Will dismounted and left his horse in the shade of a big maple tree. The boys headed for the harness shed.

"He makes me see red every time I run into him," Jim said.

"Say that again, Jim."

"I said, 'He makes me see—' "

"I thought that was what you said," Will interrupted. "No one can *make you* see red, Jim. What you mean is that you *let yourself* get mad. It's all in what goes on in your own head."

"Oh, come on, Will. Don't people make you mad sometimes?"

"Only when I let them. You don't have to let Coy *make* you do anything. Do what you please and see how he likes it. You're not one of these mules that a man can train to jump or stand still at his biddin'. You're on your way to growin' up, Jim, so take the first step. Take responsibility for yourself. Gettin' into a fist fight isn't the way to do it. Boy, I hate to think how I'd be beaten up if I let my temper rule me." He grinned at Jim and added, "That's one thing about bein' small—you learn to use your head to save your skin."

Pedro walked over to Jim and nuzzled at his hip pocket.

"Look at that," Will laughed. "He knows you have an apple in that pocket."

"Yep. Old Pedro here and I are buddies, aren't we, Pedro?"

Jim took the apple from his pocket. Pedro drew his lips back from his big teeth and gently took it from Jim's hand.

"Is he your mule?" Will asked.

"I sure wish he was," Jim said. "He belongs to Mr. Hood—but Mr. Hood lets me ride him."

"Pedro acts like you're his owner," Will said. "Well, come on. Let's get that team together and see if they've learned their lessons as well as Pedro has. And Jim, I hope you've learned a lesson about that guy Coy. Next time, call his bluff, but use your head when you do it and hold back on your temper."

That sounded all right, but just the same, Jim hoped there wouldn't be any next time. Maybe he would do as Coy wanted—maybe he'd get out of town. The idea of going with the caravan was sounding better and better.

Three days before the caravan was scheduled to leave, Mr. Hood and Jim were almost through with preparing the orders from traders. Packing materials were strewn about, and Mr. Hood suggested they do some cleaning up. Soon after they started, he pulled the saddlebags and the saddle from their resting place at the back of the store.

"Jim, what did you say was the name of the fellow who owned these? A friend of your father's, wasn't he?"

"Yes, sir. His name was Jeremiah Jones. Jeremiah had a cabin upriver a ways, and he used to come to our place a lot."

Mr. Hood was examining the saddle. "This saddle is too fine a thing to leave unused and gathering dust. You said Jones didn't have any relatives?"

"He lived alone, sir, but now that I think about it, I remember his sayin' he had a brother back east somewhere. Reckon that's all the family he had."

"Well, I doubt if that brother back east is likely to come for these things. If he does, we'll give them to him, but that's highly unlikely. Somehow, Jim, I think Jones would like his best friend's son to have them. Move them back to the storeroom by your cot. As far as I'm concerned, they're yours. You've earned them."

Jim felt happiness well up inside him. Thanks to Mr. Hood, now he really would be ready to go west, with his own saddle and saddlebags. He already had a rifle. All he needed was a horse or a mule. Like Kit said, what more did a man need?

He stood there a moment, holding the heavy saddle and saddlebags. He looked up at his employer and saw a puzzled expression on his face.

"There's something on your mind, Jim," Mr. Hood said. "Can you let me in on what's bothering you?"

Jim knew he should tell Mr. Hood about his plans—and tell him now. But he couldn't. He'd do it later. He smiled and said, "It's great to have my own saddle and saddlebags—I wish Pa was here and I could tell him about it."

Feeling a bit ashamed at losing his courage, Jim turned to his bedroom with the treasures. As he set them on his bed, he thought about the supplies in the saddlebags and how he'd be needing them when he started west. He'd just leave them in the pockets and stow the bags under the bed until it was time to pack his own things. He took a moment to admire the trimmings on the saddle again before he pushed it under the bed alongside the bags.

The pleasant clang of the dinner bell called Jim and his employer to the house, and after dinner there was plenty to keep them busy all afternoon. Jim's mind kept drifting to his plans, however. When he was waiting on one woman, he didn't even hear her order.

"Young man, aren't you listening?" she said in a sharp voice. Mr. Hood looked over from where he was attending to another customer.

"I'm sorry, Mrs. Hardy," Jim said. "How many yards shall I measure?" *Pay attention!* he told himself as he measured out five yards of calico for the woman. *Mr. Hood will be sorry he gave me the saddle.* He forced himself to keep his mind on his work the rest of the afternoon.

At supper, Jim had another surprise. "A saddle isn't much good unless you have an animal to go under it," Mr. Hood told him. "You've done a good job here for almost no pay except your meals and a place to sleep. I think you've earned more. Pick out one of my mules for your own—even Pedro, if you want him. Get yourself a saddle blanket and a bridle from the stock in the store, and you'll be all set."

Jim could hardly believe his ears. "You mean I can have Pedro for my very own, to keep?"

"That's right. He's yours to ride whenever and wherever you like, when your day's work is done. Even when you and your pa go west—although I hate to think about losing you." He stopped for a moment. Jim was having trouble sitting still at the table, and the smile on his face showed the thanks he felt. He started to speak, but Mr. Hood held up his hand.

"Remember, young man, this means that you are also responsible for taking care of him."

"Yes, sir. I'll take good care of him!"

But the guilty feeling came back to dull his happiness. Thoughts tumbled through his head. Should he tell Mr. Hood he and Pedro would be leaving, and make sure the offer still held? It wasn't fair to take the mule and not tell him—that he knew.

He was about to say something when Mr. Hood stood up and the moment was gone. "I've got some book work to do. While it's still light enough, Jim, take that wagon and team in front of the store over to the pasture lot." He smiled. "While you're there, maybe you'll want to tell Pedro he has a new owner."

9

Big Day, Big Plans

JIM's mind was awhirl as he climbed onto the wagon seat. He started the team forward but stopped when he saw Kit and Will coming across the square.

"Ride out to the pasture with me," Jim called. "I've got some news!"

As the two boys climbed into the wagon, Jim told them how Mr. Hood had rewarded him for his work.

"You sure are lucky," Kit said. "You've got everything—a good saddle, a mule, your rifle. What's to stop you from goin' to Santa Fe now?"

Will cut in, and his tone was serious. "Look, you two. You've never been out there. It's a thousand miles from the nearest United States town. You don't know what it's like. And besides being a greenhorn, there are some other things Jim should be thinkin' about. What's to stop him, Kit? Well, how about not lettin' Mr. Hood down when he's countin' on him for help? Or doin' as his father told him and stayin' right here till he hears from him? And maybe he really is too young to head out west alone, with no money and no idea what it's really like out there."

Jim and Kit were quiet for a minute. Then Jim said, "But, Will, I could always work and earn my keep, even out there, couldn't I? And Mr. Hood can find another boy to work for him. As for Pa, he could have come back or sent word to me, like he said he would. How long can I just wait around here?" He paused for a moment, then added, "Besides, I can hardly go to sleep at night worryin' about when Coy will come back again. If I don't leave Franklin when the caravan goes, I know for sure he'll come lookin' for me."

"I think he's right, Will," Kit said. "I think he should go."

Will said nothing. After an uncomfortable silence, Jim said, "You really don't think I should go, Will?"

"I told you what I think. I haven't changed my mind. But I'm not your father—or your conscience either."

They rode on to the pasture lot. Only the sight of Pedro opening his mouth in a great bray of greeting broke the strained feelings among the boys.

The next few days passed quickly. Each evening Jim saddled Pedro and took a ride, heading westward as if he was starting for Santa Fe. On the third evening, he talked quietly to his mule as he took off the saddle and got him ready to be turned loose for the night in the pasture.

"Tomorrow night we won't be comin' back here, Pedro. Tomorrow night we'll be out on the trail. Get a good rest now, and I'll see you in the mornin'." He rubbed Pedro's nose, and the mule nuzzled his shoulder in return.

The next morning, the day the caravan was to leave, Jim was wide awake before dawn. Something nagged at him, making itself felt through the excitement—he had not yet told Mr. Hood of his plans.

Except for that part, it all seemed so simple. He was to meet the Bents out at the pasture at sunrise to help harness their teams, and he would bring Pedro back and put him in the stable between the Hoods' house and the store. When the time came to slip away, Pedro would be there, and Mr. Hood would think he was just going out for his usual evening ride.

There his guilt got the better of him, and Jim felt himself breaking into a sweat even though the room was fairly cool. "I have to tell Mr. Hood that I'm goin'," he said aloud. "I'll tell him at noon—or maybe at suppertime."

For a moment he wavered. Maybe he should just tell Kit he wasn't going. He thought of what Kit would say and changed his mind again. "I'm goin'," he said as he got out of bed. The gray light was coming into the room. It was time to begin the day.

There was much to be done before breakfast, and Jim got a chunk of bread and some cheese from the Hoods' kitchen to carry him over. He ate as he walked north to the pasture. When he reached it, he climbed over the gate and stepped down onto the cool grass. Away from the fence, the ground was bare in many places, baked hard from the sun and lack of rain.

It sure would help to have a rainy day, he thought. *The men out on the trail will need good grass for the animals when they camp.* He half-smiled as he said aloud, "I mean when *we* camp. Pedro will need grass to keep him nice and sleek."

He took the pitchfork stuck into the supply of hay and threw forkloads of fodder to the animals. The mules and donkeys and horses soon came from their resting positions to feed. Jim had been putting hay out for them for two weeks because there was so little grass.

As he worked, his thoughts circled about. *How will Mr. Hood get this job done tomorrow? He can't get a new boy that soon.*

But there won't be so many animals to feed tomorrow—lots of them will leave with the caravan, he told himself. *There'll be all of Mr. Hood's breeding stock,* the nagging voice answered. *And what if a prairie fire starts in this dryness? What will Mr. Hood do without your help?*

The nagging voice stopped when something pushed against Jim's back.

"Pedro!" The black mule was nuzzling him. "Didn't I say good mornin' to you? Well, old boy, we're goin' to be together all the time from tonight on." He laid his arm over the mule's shoulder. Pedro pushed about until he found the apple in Jim's shirt pocket.

"You're a smart one, Pedro! You know I never forget to bring an apple for you. All right, here it is." He pulled out the apple, somewhat wormy but still delicious to Pedro, who crunched it noisily with his strong white teeth.

Jim checked the animals' water supply. The creek that flowed through the pasture was low, and Mr. Hood would have to move his animals soon or get someone to bring water up from the river if it didn't rain soon. *Wonder who he can get to do the work?* Back to worrying about Mr. Hood again, he noticed. He straightened up and pushed his hair back from his face.

"Why should I worry so much about Mr. Hood?" he asked aloud. "I'm not bound to him, like as if I was apprenticed. And if Pa had come back, Mr. Hood would have had to do without me—"

"Hey, Jim, who're you talkin' to? Those mules can't answer you!" It was Will Bent, calling out as he climbed over the gate.

Just then, one of the mules opened his mouth wide, and a loud bray cut through the morning stillness. Both boys laughed.

"See? Mules are good listeners, and they even talk back sometimes," Jim said. One of the little donkeys standing nearby chose that moment to give a resounding "Heehaw!"

The boys were still laughing when Charles Bent came over the gate, as lithe as his younger brother. "Sounds like a good joke goin' on over here. That's the way to start a busy day."

"Mornin', Mr. Bent," Jim said. "Your teams are fed and ready to be harnessed. We can start them toward the square in just a few minutes."

He brought the Bents' eight mules into a small corral near the gate. Charles had brought harnesses with him so that he and Will could walk the teams back to the square and hitch them to the two new wagons he had bought to take west. The three worked at getting the bridles and harness into place.

"Do you need any more boys to help with the animals on the trail, Mr. Bent?" Jim was standing near Charles when he asked this question.

The look that he got in response made him feel that Charles knew exactly what he had in mind.

"Hmm," he said in reply. A mule tossed its head as he was trying to slip the bridle into place. "Steady, boy. Easy there," Charles soothed, then finished getting the bridle on.

He stepped back and took off his hat to scratch his head a moment. Jim fidgeted, waiting for an answer while Charles pushed his dark hair back and put his hat on. He looked closely at Jim.

"What do you have in mind?" he asked.

"I'm thinkin' I'll head west," Jim answered casually. "A friend and I want to leave tonight, right after the caravan goes." Jim was sure that Charles knew who the friend was.

"Well, we can always use a couple of good hands with the animals," Charles said, "but I want you to think about somethin'. Will told me about your situation, with your father not returnin' when you expected him to. Let me tell you this—if I were your father, I'd expect you to stay on the job with Mr. Hood until such time as you heard from me. I wouldn't want a fifteen-year-old son of mine to start west on some wild goose chase tryin' to find me."

"But, Mr. Bent, there hasn't been any word from him, and I think I know where he is. He might have told Jeremiah Jones to see that I got started on this caravan."

Charles said nothing, so Jim went on.

"I may be only fifteen, but I'm tall and pretty strong, and I know how to take care of myself. I've got a mule, a saddle, and a rifle, and I know how to handle animals. Kit and I would look for Mr. Kincaid—the one who had the fort here—when we got out there. He'd know how I could find Pa."

"Kit? So he's the friend. Well, he's a good boy. He'll be all right—he's got his older brothers to help him. What do they think of his goin'?"

Jim felt he had betrayed his friend, even if by accident. "Please, Mr. Bent—I swore to Kit I wouldn't tell about his goin'. His brothers don't know. Please don't give him away!"

"I won't say anything—I guessed it, anyway. For him, it will work out all right. But for you . . . if Mr. Hood felt it was right for you to go, Jim, I'd be all for it. I'd have a job for you. But I want you to think it over. Mr. Hood has treated you well, hasn't he?"

"Yes, sir." Jim's thoughts were all tangled up. What *would* Pa want him to do? And Ma, if she were alive? The nagging voice inside him spoke again. *You know very well both of them would tell you to do what is right—and what is right is to stay here.*

"And get beaten up again," Jim muttered aloud.

"What did you say?" Charles asked.

Jim's face turned red. "That guy Colton said he'd beat me up again if I didn't get out of town."

"Is that the real reason you're plannin' to leave?" Charles asked. "Don't answer that." He turned to go. "Let's get these teams on the road. Open the gate, Jim."

Jim fastened one last buckle on the harness and hurried to open the big gate, watching as Charles and Will started their teams toward the town square. He had more mules to deliver to other buyers; then he would follow on Pedro.

Is it really because I'm scared of Coy that I decided to go? Jim asked himself. After a moment he answered, *I'm goin' with Kit, no matter what!*

It was nearly the middle of the morning when he was ready to go back to town. He hadn't brought his saddle, but he could ride Pedro home bareback, even without a bridle. They started out after he closed the gate, but Jim didn't feel as happy or excited as he had expected.

Back at the Hoods', he put Pedro into a stall and patted the mule's neck. "Be ready, Pedro. We leave tonight. If we don't, we'll have to stay all winter."

He went into the store by way of the back door. Everything he would take with him was in the storeroom—his saddle, rifle, powder horn, flint, sack of bullets and wadding, and the things in the saddlebags. He'd add his extra clothes and be ready to go. Mr. Hood wouldn't mind if he left his mother's trunk here for now. He'd bring some bread from the house at dinnertime so that he and Kit would have some food until they could get some game or fish.

He could hear voices in the store. Knowing that Mr. Hood must be very busy and in need of his help, he went on through.

"I'm back, Mr. Hood!" he called. "What do you want me to do first?"

"You're just in time to help Mr. Bent get his merchandise from the warehouse, Jim." Charles was standing there, his arms loaded with bolts of cloth. "Help him get these things into his wagon, then go with him down to the warehouse to get the things on this list. Here's the key."

Charles led the way to the big freight wagon Jim had seen when the Bent brothers arrived in Franklin. The canvas cover was open to make the loading easier. Other wagons and teams were in the square, too, along with many pack mules. Men were working to get everything ready for the departure.

Jim climbed up onto the wagon seat, alongside Charles. After a moment, Charles said, "Well, Jim, have you decided what you're goin' to do?"

"Yes, sir. But I promise I won't leave without tellin' Mr. Hood. Kit and I will start after dark, after we both finish our day's work."

Charles sat quietly for a moment. Then he said, "It's your decision. I don't agree with you, but look me up when you and Kit catch up to the caravan. I'll have work for you until we reach the Cimarron crossing. You and Kit will have to earn your keep another way after that, when the rest of the caravan crosses the river to go on to Santa Fe."

"Thanks, Mr. Bent. I don't think you'll be sorry."

"I wish I could say the same to you. One thing—remember that's a promise about tellin' Mr. Hood before you leave."

"Yes, sir. I promise."

They stopped the wagon alongside the big door of the warehouse. Jim jumped down and went around to unlock the small door. As he put the key into the keyhole, he was glad he wasn't alone this time. There was still a dark ring around his eye to remind him of the day Coy had followed him here.

Soon the two of them were hauling out bolts of cloth and some of the other goods Charles would need for Indian gifts and fur-trading when he reached the upper Arkansas River.

"Will you be buildin' your tradin' post fort this winter, Mr. Bent?" Jim asked.

"No, but we may find the right location for it. This trip will help us decide if wagons can travel the new route easily, and what the prospects are for good trade."

Jim smiled. "Maybe Pa and I will be bringin' packs of furs to you. We can help each other get rich!"

Charles grinned. "Maybe so, Jim. Maybe there will be a Bent's Fort out there soon, and trappers will be tickled pink to see it when they come down from a winter in the mountains. Maybe you and your father—and Kit Carson, too—will be among them."

He was arranging the merchandise in the wagon. Straightening up, he said, "We'd better go over to Bernard's and get some more rope. If I don't tie this stuff down, I'll be in trouble when we cross those little streams out on the plains."

They checked the list once more and closed up the warehouse. Then Charles called to Jim from the wagon seat. "While I'm gettin' rope, Jim, will you do an errand for me? There's no place out on the Arkansas River that sells cigars—so could you go get me three boxes to take along?"

"Yes, sir." Charles gave Jim some Spanish silver to pay for the cigars. As he passed the tobacco factory, Jim noticed a farm wagon at the door and a familiar figure unloading a crop of tobacco leaves. It was young Caleb Bingham, bringing tobacco from the family farm near the Arrow Rock ferry.

"Hey, Caleb!" Jim called. "Glad I ran into you. I've got somethin' to tell you, and a favor to ask."

Caleb jumped down from the wagon. "I've got somethin' to tell you, too, Jim Mathews. You should have seen how mad that guy Colton was after you hit him at the tavern! I thought he was goin' to explode, and I was afraid he'd be after me, too, for blockin' his way. Did he catch up with you?"

Then Caleb saw the dark ring around Jim's eye and some of the bruises now turning green.

"Not that night," Jim answered, "but you should have seen me when he did. It was the Monday night after the goose pull, and he was double-mad by then 'cause he thought I cheated him out of gettin' the goose."

"Boy, I'll bet you think twice before you hit a big guy like that again! What were you goin' to tell me?"

"Wait a minute while I go in and buy some cigars for Mr. Bent."

When he came out, the two boys walked toward the river and sat down on a driftwood log. Jim could see Mr. Bent's wagon from where he sat.

"Caleb, will you do a couple of old pals a favor? Kit and I are headin' west tonight after dark—"

"You're *what?*" Caleb jumped up. "You mean you and Kit are runnin' away with the caravan?"

"Hey, keep it quiet! Yeah—somethin' like that. Kit's runnin' away. I'm just goin' to meet my father. Anyway, Kit has to stay hidden until it's safe to be seen so Mr. Workman won't catch him and bring him back."

Caleb's round eyes were even rounder than usual. "You mean you guys are leavin' for keeps? All the way west?"

"Don't you tell anyone!"

"I won't. Well, what's the favor?"

"I sure hope you can do it, Caleb—it will be after dark, and the ferry won't be operatin'. We've got to get across the Missouri. If we try to cross farther up the river in daylight, we might get caught."

"Likely so. But I don't run a ferry, Jim."

"No, but you've got a boat, haven't you?"

Caleb nodded. "Yes, but I brought the tobacco wagon over by ferry. My boat's at home, on the other side of the river."

"Well, here's the favor—and it's a big one, Caleb. Would you row across to the north bank at Arrow Rock tonight after dark and wait for Kit and me to meet you there? We'll get there as quick as we can."

Caleb's eyes sparkled and his round face beamed. "Just like spies—real secret? Sure, Jim. I couldn't do it if the river was high like it was last spring, but it's low right now, 'specially at the ferry crossin'. I'll be there—promise!"

"There's Mr. Bent," Jim said, standing up. "I've got to go now. Bring a lantern, Caleb—there won't be much moonlight. And thanks, pal. See you tonight!"

He picked up the cigars and ran. His plans were all set.

10

The Caravan Leaves

By afternoon, the preparations were complete. On the square, most of the wagons stood loaded and waiting for the teams to be hitched. A line of pack animals, each with two large bundles tied in place, stood ready to start, while a few more stood waiting for the packers.

Jim sat on the edge of the boardwalk watching two men load a mule. They were doing the work Mexican-style, placing the two bundles on the ground, one on each side of the animal.

One of the men put a sheepskin, covered by a saddle cloth, on the mule's back to protect it from the rubbing of the load. Jim could see, however, that this pack mule was still sore from a strap that had scraped its hind legs on an earlier journey. When the other packer tried to place the saddle, with the crupper strap attached to it, on the animal's back, the mule suddenly brayed. It tossed its head and tried to break loose.

"*Basta! Alto, alto!*" the packer commanded. The man grasped the mule's halter to hold him still.

"He'll have to wear blinders," the other man said, and found the small squares of soft leather to put over the mule's eyes. He tied them into place and the mule quieted immediately. The man with the saddle went on with his work. It was a Mexican pack saddle—not a wooden frame, but a square of leather, doubled and stuffed with straw to make it stand out at the lower sides. The Mexicans called it an *aparejo.*

"Uunh-naa-aay!" brayed the mule as the man on the animal's left put his knee against his ribs and gave a great pull to tighten the cinch that held the saddle in place.

Poor thing, Jim thought. *I don't see how it can breathe. I wouldn't want Pedro to be a pack mule.*

The load went on next. Each man picked up a bundle, and in a short while they had a coil of rope around it to hold it in place on the saddle. Around and around went the rope, as tightly bound as the cinch.

"*Adios!*" yelled the man who had tied the last knots. At this signal, the other man slipped off the blinders.

"*Vaya!*" he said, and gave the mule a slap on the rump at the same time. "*Anda!*" The mule trotted off obediently to take its place in the long line.

"Those mules know more Spanish than I do," someone said in Jim's ear. Kit had taken a place beside him.

"Yeah. Guess we'll have to learn a few words ourselves. I've been studyin' how they put the packs on—you and I might have to help load, you know, when we catch up."

"Likely we will. Are you all set for tonight? I'm gettin' pretty excited."

"Me, too. I got it worked out how we're goin' to cross the river."

"I was wonderin' about that," Kit said. "We can't cross on the ferry tomorrow. Workman's would send someone after me, and that would be the end of the whole thing— for me, anyway."

"Caleb's helpin' us. I saw him this mornin', and he'll bring his boat across after dark, at Arrow Rock. We can load our stuff in the boat, saddles and all, and just leave the bridles on the mules. The river's so low the mules can walk part of the way, and we can make 'em swim where it gets deep."

"Only thing is, I ain't got a mule."

Jim was dismayed. "I thought you were goin' to borrow one from one of your brothers."

Kit shook his head. "Can't seem to get one without givin' away the secret. They'd know right away what I was up to. And no one else would let me borrow one—I haven't even asked, 'cause they'd only ask questions."

"Well, we'll just have to take turns ridin'. It'll take a long time to catch up to the caravan, though."

Just then they heard the long signal call. "They're ready to start," Kit said. They ran to a place where they could watch the line of wagons, pack mules, and riders leave the square.

"There's Robert," Kit said. "William's got a wagon, but Robert and Ham are takin' pack mules."

Robert Carson's mules were not very far back in the line, and Ham's were right behind. Each had eight pack animals, plus a mule on which he was riding and a spare mule following.

Kit ran out to walk beside Robert, making one last try. "Please let me go, Robert! Let me ride your spare. We can send word back to Ma that I'm with you. I'll come back when you do. She won't mind—"

The tall young man on the mule looked like a giant above his smaller brother. He grinned down at Kit and poked him with the toe of his boot. "You're a good talker, Kit, with that doggone smile of yours. But you know I can't do that. Next year will be different—you'll see. Ma'll let you go with her blessin'."

For a moment, Kit was tempted to release the spare mule and keep it to ride later. But the group moved on, and he called out, "So long, Robert. So long, Ham. See you." He turned away.

"So long, shorty."

Kit stood beside Jim, and the boys watched as the caravan moved on.

"Ham don't know just how soon he's gonna see me," Kit said.

"You don't think they've guessed?"

"No. How 'bout Mr. Hood? Have you told him you're goin'?"

"No—I've been tryin' to find the right time, but I just can't seem to tell him. I will. I'll tell him when I go to supper tonight."

"You ain't backin' out, are you?"

"Not likely! But I know Mr. Hood will try to talk me into stayin'."

The wagons were passing now. "Here comes William," Kit said. He ran out to the road. "William, please let me go with you. I'll help with the drivin'!"

Kit's oldest half brother smiled down at the boy who was more like a son than a brother to him. "No, Kit. See you when I get back. And remember to go out to the farm to see Ma as often as you can."

Kit and Jim watched for the Bents' wagons at the end of the line. Charles and Will were riding their horses; hired men handled the teams. Jim was pleased to see the mules he had helped to train were behaving well.

Charles waved and rode by, but Will left the line and stopped for a moment. "See you out on the trail?" he asked in a low voice.

"You sure will," Kit said. "But for show, let's say our good-byes." He reached up to shake Will's hand, then said good-bye loud enough for others to hear. Jim did the same.

"We might have to lay low and stay behind for a few days." Kit added. "In case anyone checks the caravan lookin' for me, Will, remember, you don't know nothin' about this."

"Cross my heart." Will smiled. "No one will get anythin' out of me. Gotta go, guys. So long!" He moved his horse back to the line.

Kit and Jim watched a few minutes longer and then turned back toward the square.

"I'd better get back to Workmans' now," Kit said. "Where will we meet tonight?"

"Sit in front of the Square and Compass. I'll ride by. If all's well, I'll just wave as I go by and keep goin'. When you're in the clear, come along as fast as you can."

"Think anyone will ask how come I've got all my gear with me?" Kit asked.

"Wait till it's real dark, and stow it 'round the corner of the inn, where you can get to it easy. I'll go halfway down the block and wait for you."

"That should work. Just be sure you show up!"

"I will—don't worry. And bring along somethin' to eat."

As Kit started to walk away, he thought of one more thing. "Don't let the Hoods talk you out of goin'—and be sure they don't give me away."

The boys parted. Soon Jim was back at the store, hoping that the excitement he felt wouldn't show on his face.

"What do you want me to do first, Mr. Hood?" he asked.

Robert Hood had also watched the departure of the caravan. He and Jim entered the store together, and he shook his head at the mess they saw there. On the floor were short ends of rope and cord, trails of spilled coffee beans and salt, and scraps of other odds and ends. There were many empty shelves, showing the great quantities of merchandise that had been moved out.

"You sweep the floor while I wipe the shelves. We'll get a fresh start before we stock up again."

A sinking feeling went through Jim. He still couldn't bring himself to speak of his plans or to tell Mr. Hood he wouldn't be around to help restock the shelves.

When the sweeping and cleaning were finished, Jim helped take inventory. They made a list of what was needed to fill orders for the army post upriver and the trade downriver before winter closed the boat traffic.

"Jim-boy, you'd make a fine merchant," Mr. Hood said toward the end of the day. "You'll make a good living here in Franklin."

Jim's guilt was getting the better of him, and Mr. Hood's calling him by the name his father used made it worse. He began telling him of his plans.

"Mr. Hood, don't count on me too much. I really want to go west to be with my pa. That's where all the excitement is."

Mr. Hood sighed. "I know what you mean, boy. Sometimes I think if I didn't have a family and a good business here, I might go west myself. I expect you'll be going in a year or so?"

There was silence for a moment. Jim swallowed hard and then said, "Mr. Hood, I—" He stopped.

"What, Jim?"

"Nothin'." The words must be stuck down deep, he thought. He'd wait until supper. Besides, Martha was out there at the well, and he couldn't leave without telling her good-bye. This would be his last chance.

"Mr. Hood, may I go and help Martha with her water bucket?"

"Sure, go ahead. Carry it home for her. I'm about through in here. I think I'll sort out those barrels in the yard while I'm waiting for Mrs. Hood to ring the supper bell. Don't be too long."

A minute later Jim stood beside Martha.

"Let me pull up that bucket."

"Thanks, Jim, that's real nice. Did you watch the caravan leave?"

"Sure did. Kit and I took a little time off to say goodbye to his brothers and to Charles and Will Bent."

Jim had the heavy bucket out of the well and the rope unhooked. Water dripped and sloshed a bit as they started toward Martha's house.

After a moment Jim said, "Martha, there's somethin' I've got to tell you, but you have to swear to keep it a secret."

Martha's eyes widened. She made a crossing movement with her hand. "Cross my heart and hope to die."

"Kit and I are runnin' away tonight—or rather, Kit's runnin' away and I'm goin' with him. We're gonna follow the caravan."

Martha stopped walking. She turned to face Jim, hands on her hips. The look on her face made him feel very small.

"Jim Mathews! It's bad enough for Kit to go when his mother asked him not to and his brothers told him to wait. But at least he knows that his brothers can give him a little help when he needs it. And besides, he's nearly seventeen. But you! You'd do this to Mr. Hood after all he's done for you?"

"Well, I'm gonna tell him before I go," he said lamely. He set down the heavy bucket. "He can get another boy to help him."

"It just isn't right, Jim! I suppose you're even gonna take Pedro. You know Mr. Hood thought you'd be here all winter when he gave Pedro to you."

"He said Pedro was mine to do with as I liked. And when I asked him if that meant I could take him west, he said yes. He said I'd earned him." Jim felt his arguments getting weaker with every word. "I'm beginnin' to be sorry I told you, Martha."

"I should think you'd be even sorrier that you'd do such a thing! You know your father told you to stay here till he came back—or sent word to you."

"Yes, but he didn't come back. And he didn't send word."

"How do you know?"

"Martha, no one—"

"What about Jeremiah Jones—don't you think he had a message for you?"

"Maybe he did, but Jeremiah's dead!"

"Well, don't blame your father for that!"

Jim had been looking down at the clean spots on his feet where the water had splashed away the dust. He looked up at Martha. Her eyes were blazing, her lips tightly closed.

"I wouldn't have told you, Martha, if I thought you were gonna be so angry."

"I suppose you'd have just sneaked off. And you say Kit's runnin' away but you're not. You're runnin' away from more than he is, and you know it. What do you think your father would say if he knew you were startin' off on such a wild goose chase? I know what he'd say— he'd say you'd lost what little good sense you had." She paused a moment, and Jim thought the scolding had ended. But then she went on.

"You're not even sixteen years old. You may be tall, but you're not ready to hold your own against grown men, and maybe even Indians out there. Why, you've still got marks from your tangle with Coy!"

Jim rubbed one foot over the other, smearing the clean spots. "Well, that's another reason to go. Coy tellin' me to get out of town."

"So you'd do it—just 'cause that bully told you to. When are you gonna think for yourself? You don't have to let him push you around. Just use your head—surely you're smarter than that big oaf!"

Jim could feel his face getting red.

"You're runnin' out on everybody, Jim—your pa, Mr. Hood, and yourself!"

"Martha, you don't understand—"

"I understand more than you think. Runnin' off sounds like more fun than stayin' here and workin' till the right time comes to leave. Well, good luck. I'll carry this bucket the rest of the way myself, thank you!"

She picked it up so quickly that water splashed onto her feet. She walked away, leaning to one side with the weight of the load.

Jim stared at the puddle in the dust. After a minute he said aloud, "I don't care what she thinks—I'm goin' anyway."

He walked slowly back to the store. In about two hours it would be time to leave, and he still had to get his things packed. No one was in the front part of the store, and he walked to the storeroom.

Looking out the window, he could see Mr. Hood in the yard climbing onto an upended barrel, apparently about to check those stacked behind it. Jim reached under the bed and pulled out the saddle. It looked as handsome as ever, but he sighed as he stooped again to get the saddlebags. Martha had taken all the excitement and fun out of his plans.

Too bad these old bags don't match the beautiful leather of the saddle, he thought as he put them on the bed. *I don't care what Martha thinks,* he fumed inwardly. He pulled out Jeremiah's old trousers and other things, emptying half of the bags. But, as he placed his own spare shirt and trousers on the bed with Jeremiah's things, he knew he really did care. He felt more sad than anything else, and the memory of his mother added to it. The shirt was the last one she had made for him.

His shoes—his only pair—were under the bed. He hadn't had them on his feet for months. He got them out and looked at them.

They'll be too tight for me, but maybe I can trade for a bigger pair—or a pair of boots. He put them alongside the moccasins he'd taken from Jeremiah's bag and saw that the moccasins were his size. He'd be glad to have them when the weather turned colder—which would be soon enough.

He shook out Jeremiah's trousers and held them up against his own. *Might have to roll up the legs just a bit, but I can use 'em,* he decided. As he started to fold them for packing, he saw something in one of the pockets.

"What's this?" he said aloud, and pulled out a piece of paper, folded twice. Just then there was a loud crash from out in the yard, the rumble of rolling barrels, and a great shout from Mr. Hood. He pushed the paper back into the pocket and ran outside.

11

Jim Takes Charge

ONE glance told Jim what had happened. Mr. Hood's foot had gone through the weathered bottom of an upended empty barrel. Now he lay struggling on the ground, his right leg caught in the overturned barrel.

"Jim, help me!" he shouted.

Jim and Mrs. Hood reached him at the same time. "Oh, Robert, are you hurt?" Mrs. Hood knelt beside her husband.

Mr. Hood's mouth was tight, his face pale. "I'm afraid so, Laura."

Jim was studying the hole where Mr. Hood's leg was stuck. "Do you think we can free him?" Mrs. Hood asked.

Jim moved around to a position where he could grasp the barrel. "Hold him up a little." he said.

While Mrs. Hood tried to lift her husband gently, Jim began to move the barrel.

"Oh—no, Jim! Please don't pull at it," Mr. Hood said.

Jim got up. "I'm going for Dr. Lowry. Hold tight, and I'll be back as quick as I can."

Mr. and Mrs. Hood watched helplessly as Jim ran to the stable for Pedro. In a minute he had freed the halter rein and backed the mule from the stall. He leaped onto Pedro's back and dug his heels into the animal's sides. Pedro broke into a gallop.

It took only a minute to get to the Lowry home. Jim jumped down from Pedro and ran to the back door. He figured the family would be at supper.

"Dr. Lowry, Dr. Lowry!" Jim called as he knocked on the door. Old Emily was in the kitchen.

"Well, land sakes, Jim Mathews, what you need the doctor for in such a hurry?" she asked.

"It's Mr. Hood. He fell and he's hurt. Where's the doctor?"

Dr. Lowry came into the kitchen, followed by Martha and Mrs. Lowry.

"Did you say Robert is hurt?"

"Yes, sir. I think he might have broken his leg, or maybe even his back. He's out in his yard and we can't move him."

"I'm on my way just as quick as I can get my bag," the doctor said, and disappeared.

"Martha and I will come along, too, Jim," Mrs. Lowry said. "Tell Mrs. Hood we'll be there in just a few minutes."

The Lowry horse was still hitched to the lightweight buggy the doctor used to make his rounds. Dr. Lowry went out the front door of the house and got into the carriage as Jim left the yard on Pedro. He reached the Hoods' just ahead of the doctor. There was a grassy area near the stable, and he left Pedro there.

"The doctor's right behind me, Mrs. Hood," he called as he ran back to where she was still kneeling beside her husband. "Mrs. Lowry and Martha will be over to help in a few minutes."

Dr. Lowry's buggy pulled into the drive alongside the house, and in a moment the doctor was with Mr. Hood. He felt the leg as best he could with most of it hidden inside the barrel, then asked some questions while checking for a back injury. After a few minutes, he stood up. "We're lucky—his back isn't injured, but likely he's broken some bones in his leg or ankle. We'll have to enlarge the hole in the barrel. Can you get some tools, Jim— maybe a crowbar and a hammer? We'll see if we can get the boards pried out, or split and pulled away."

Jim was off to the shed where tools were kept. Pedro was feeding on the grass. He looked up as Jim came near, and then went back to grazing.

It took some time for Jim to pry loose the board next to the one that had broken. He was afraid to push or pull very hard, for fear of hurting Mr. Hood even more. The doctor helped by holding the injured leg as best he could.

"There!" Jim said at last. With the board removed, he was able to pull the barrel out of the way. Dr. Lowry examined the leg for injuries. "What on earth did you think you were doing, Robert?" he asked. "Not satisfied with being a merchant, you've got to start a circus and be your own acrobat?"

Mr. Hood smiled weakly. "I was testing the empty barrels to see if they were sound enough to use again. I found out about this one the hard way."

"I think even Pedro would have had better sense, Robert," Dr. Lowry responded. "Jim, I'm going to need your help. We have a bone-setting job to do. But first, help me carry him inside."

Mrs. Hood led the way to the house as Jim and Dr. Lowry, hands clasped to make a support for Mr. Hood, carried the injured man inside and to a couch. For the next hour Jim was busy riding back to Dr. Lowry's house for supplies and helping the doctor with the work. Martha and her mother had arrived just as they were carrying Mr. Hood into the house. Martha said nothing to Jim directly. She and her mother helped Mrs. Hood finish preparing the supper.

When his work was finished and Mr. Hood's leg was in its splints, Dr. Lowry packed his bag. "You made a good assistant, Jim," he said. "How about planning to study medicine? I'd be interested in having you work with me."

A feeling of pleasure swept through Jim, even though he doubted he would ever want to become a doctor. He sat down with the rest of the group to eat a little supper.

It was then that his thoughts returned to his own concerns for the first time since the accident. He glanced out the window and saw that it was already dark. Kit! Kit would be waiting for him over at the Square and Compass! He took a spoonful of soup, then another, and put his spoon down. He moved uneasily in his chair and saw that Dr. Lowry was looking at him.

"What makes you so quiet, Jim?"

For a moment, Jim didn't answer. Then he said, "I've had some things on my mind, Dr. Lowry." He turned to speak to Mrs. Hood and caught Martha staring at him. "Mrs. Hood, may I be excused?" he asked. "I'm really not hungry, and there were some things I was goin' to take care of. I left Pedro out there, and it's already dark."

"Of course, Jim," Mrs. Hood said. "Your soup can be warmed up again. And thank you for all your help. I'd have been lost without you tonight."

As Jim got up, his eyes met Martha's. She's waiting for me to tell Mr. Hood, he thought, and felt the scorn in her glance. He turned away.

Mr. Hood called to him from the couch, "Lock up the store for me, Jim—give him the key, please, Laura." Mrs. Hood got the big door key from her husband and gave it to Jim.

"I'll have to count on you for many things until Robert is back on his feet," she said, smiling. "You and I will be his legs for a while. Go along now."

With the caravan gone and the town so quiet, he decided he'd lock up the store after he got back—he'd be gone only a few minutes. He whistled for Pedro, who came immediately.

"Let's go, Pedro," Jim said as he jumped on his back. "We've some business to take care of."

He rode at a walk away from the house and turned west toward the Square and Compass. Through the darkness he could see Kit's stocky form leaning against the corner post of the porch.

No one else seemed to be around, and he called Kit's name softly as he rode by. He looked to the right as he left the square, and saw three figures mounted on mules or horses approaching from the north. He urged Pedro into a dark side street and, looking back, saw Kit following. Kit was carrying a big bundle, his saddle, and his rifle.

Jim was well hidden by the shadows of the leafy roadside trees when he stopped to wait for Kit. He heard a loud laughing and voices coming from the square, and he could see the riders had arrived.

Just what I need, he thought. *Coy Colton and his buddies—what a night!*

He decided to move on a little farther so that he and Kit would not be seen. Kit followed at a distance. When he was sure they would be safe, he stopped and dismounted. Pedro brayed a little.

"Quiet, Pedro. Everything's all right."

At last Kit came up to him, struggling under the weight of his gear. "I'm glad you made it," he said, dropping his burden. "But wait a minute—you don't have your saddle or saddlebags, or even your rifle. What's wrong?"

"I can't go."

Kit stared at him. After a pause, Jim told him what had happened. "I just can't let them down. I'll have to wait until the next caravan goes."

"But that won't be until spring," Kit protested. "That means we sit here all winter—"

"For me, that's what it means," Jim said. "But you can go ahead. Someone's got to tell Caleb, anyway. Likely he's rowing his way to this side of the river right now, and it will take you an hour to get up there. You've got to go alone, Kit, and you'd better get started."

"You know what's waitin' for you when you go back to the store, Jim? Coy Colton's been talkin' around. He says if you don't leave town today, he'll make you so sorry you won't be able to go nowhere. Didn't you see him comin' to the square just now?"

"Yeah, I saw him. I'll keep out of his way goin' back." Jim smiled. "Shake hands, old buddy. I'll sure miss you. Send word back with someone you meet on the trail and let me know how things are goin'."

Kit slung his bundle over his shoulder and picked up his heavy saddle and the rifle. He looked as if he'd never make it to Arrow Rock.

"Sure wish you'd found a mule to borrow," Jim said. He put his arm up over Pedro's shoulder and studied his friend. "Look, Kit—I'll let you borrow Pedro. But just till you catch up with the caravan, mind you! Then you send him on back to me. If you don't meet anyone who can bring him back, leave him at Fort Osage for him to be shipped downriver to Franklin by boat. I'll pay whoever brings him back, somehow or other."

"You really mean that, Jim?" Kit's voice was wondering and joyful at the same time. "You'll let me borrow Pedro? Boy, I'll sure see that he starts back home for you. You're the best!" He was already undoing his bundle and getting his saddle and gear separated. It took very little time for him to have Pedro saddled, his bundle tied in place, and himself mounted and ready to go.

Jim was rubbing Pedro's nose. "Be careful of him when you're crossin' the river," he said to Kit. "I'll start watchin' for him in about a week. Won't have any time for ridin' this week, anyway. . . ." Something caught in Jim's throat and he had to stop talking. He watched as Kit took up the reins, and his heart felt like a lead weight.

"Jim, you're the greatest. If I don't come back before you head west, you ask David Kincaid for me out there.

He'll know where to find me—and we'll trap together. So long!"

In a moment, mule and rider had disappeared in the darkness. Jim had never felt so alone, not even when his pa had gone away after his mother died. When he could see his best friend and his mule no longer, he stood looking after them for a moment, then turned back toward the square.

I've gotta lock up the store, he suddenly remembered, and began to run. As he reached the square, he slowed a moment to see where Coy and his friends had gone. There were no horses tied outside the Union Hall or the Square and Compass; it was an unusually quiet night. On the south side of the square there was some activity—loud voices came from a tavern, and some animals were tied outside.

That looks like Coy's mule, Jim thought. *I hope he stays there.*

There were no lights on in the store. Jim went in through the front door and closed it behind him. He fitted the key into the lock, turned it, and dropped the bar into place. *I'd better bar up the back door, too,* he told himself. *Mr. Hood can't come and help me if that gang comes again tonight.*

As he made his way back toward the storeroom in the darkness, there were shuffling sounds off to the left. Jim grinned.

The mice won't find much to eat around here tonight, he thought, laughing to himself. *We swept things out too well.* He was about to go to bed when he remembered he hadn't finished his supper—and that his bed would have to be cleared, for the saddle and the things he had been packing were still on it. He groped in the darkness for a bit of tinder and his flint and steel, which he kept on the box beside his bed.

Then he remembered. *That paper in Jeremiah's trouser pocket! It could be a note from Pa!* He fumbled with the flint, trying to get a spark as he struck it against the little piece of steel. His hands shook, and he tried four times before the tinder began to burn at last and he could light the candle wick. Hastily, he smothered the tinder flame as the candlelight glowed, and he put the candle safely into its holder on the box.

For a moment he thought about barring the back door first, but he wanted to see if the paper was from his pa. That paper might be the only bright spot in his day—he had to find out now. He picked up the trousers and pulled the paper from the pocket.

"Got you this time, Beanpole!" The voice came from the doorway leading into the store.

Jim nearly jumped out of his skin. Coy had been hiding in the darkness of the store when he walked through! No doubt his buddies were right behind him. A shuffling of feet proved this.

"You just stand right where you are," Coy said. For one long moment, Coy looked him over from head to foot. Then he shook his head. "So you didn't have enough sense to follow my advice." He waited to let this sink in. Then he said, "Now you'll have to be punished."

Jim could only stare. The shadows of the candlelight made Coy's face grotesque, like the faces of ugly creatures Jim had imagined when his mother used to read old folktales to him long ago. Strange that he should think of that now, with all he was facing. But the creatures had come to bad ends in the stories; how could he end this story?

To his own surprise, he felt quite calm. He could almost hear Will Bent's voice: *He can't make you do anything. Use your head to save your skin.*

"Scared, ain'tcha, Beanpole?" Coy said. "You should be."

Jim noticed the flour dust in Coy's hair. In the candlelight, it made him look like an old man. He realized that he wasn't scared—he was smarter than Coy and his buddies. Whatever happened, he was going to hold off the attack that soon would come. He thrust the paper, still folded, into his pants pocket to free his hands.

"My, my," Coy taunted, "it looks like Daddy's little beanpole was packin' to go somewhere. Was he goin' to take the beautiful saddle? Too bad he didn't go earlier. When we get through, I'll take the saddle home with me."

Jim stood waiting for Coy to make the first move. He said nothing.

Coy hesitated. Then he said, "First, before I pound the daylights out o' you, pull that there piece o' paper outa your pocket. I'll read it 'n' see if it's all right for a little boy to read." He was using his syrupy voice, the same one that had so angered Jim before.

Jim did not move.

"So—I'll have to take it from you." Coy stepped forward. His two pals appeared in the shadowy doorway behind him. Coy grabbed Jim's shoulder with his left hand, raising his right arm threateningly. His face close to Jim's, he said, "Come on now, pull out that paper!"

Jim saw Coy's yellow teeth and smelled the unwashed body and the whiskey on his breath. Instead of reaching for the paper, Jim thrust his foot forward quickly, trying to hook it around Coy's leg to throw him off balance.

Coy saw the move, let go of Jim's shoulder, and stepped aside in time. "Now you'll get it, Mathews!" he snarled. "I'm tired of playin' with you!"

He sent his fist toward Jim's face. Jim ducked and took the blow as it glanced off his shoulder. Coy swung again, and this time his aim was truer. It caught Jim in the chest, and he fell back against the saddle on his cot. As he fell, he grabbed at Coy to bring him down with him.

Coy staggered, knocking against the upended box Jim used as a table. The box tipped over, and the candle lay on the floor, its wax making a pool in which the flame spread.

"Look out!" Jim cried when he saw the spreading flame. "You're settin' the place on fire!" He pushed Coy to one side and pulled his spare trousers from the cot where they lay ready to be packed. Coy gazed stupidly at the spreading flame that traveled along now in the dry splintery wood of the floor.

Jim dropped to his knees, trying to smother the flame with the trousers. He had to stop its spread before it went any farther! A keg of gunpowder stood by the doorway where Coy's buddies stood like two statues.

Then suddenly Coy came to life. "Let the place burn! I'm gettin' that saddle and I'm gonna beat you up so you'll never walk again. Get out in the yard!"

Coy grabbed the saddle and kicked at Jim, who was still trying to smother the flame. Jim rolled out of the way and got to his feet just in time to see one of Coy's buddies holding the little keg of gunpowder over his head. He was going to hurl it at Jim. "I'll get him, Coy!" the boy yelled. "This'll knock his brains out!"

Jim cried, "That's gunpowder!" Like a panther, he leaped toward the boy holding the keg. Jim was taller than the boy, and as he jumped he reached to push the keg back toward the open doorway, away from the fire. The boy fell backward, and the keg rolled away into the store.

Jim turned back to the flames. Now they were really spreading. The third boy, frightened, had run out into the yard through the back door. A breeze came into the room through the open door and fanned the creeping flames.

Coy stood motionless, still holding the saddle, seemingly dazed. Jim had time to think. He pushed Coy to the door.

"Get out of here before you burn up! And stay out of my way!"

He gave no thought to the saddle as Coy stumbled out the door, still carrying it. Quickly, Jim pulled the blanket from his bed. Jeremiah's clothing and Jim's extra shirt came with it, and the boy used all of them to fight the flames. He didn't hear Dr. Lowry's voice, shouting from out in the yard, nor the women calling his name. He was desperately beating at the fringes of the flame with his hands when he felt a splash of water and heard sizzling as it hit the fire.

"Jim!" Dr. Lowry was pulling him up. "Get out before you burn yourself up!"

Jim got up and backed off as Dr. Lowry poured water on the floor. He had Jim's water bucket from the bench outside the door. "Get the water bucket from the house, Martha!" he yelled, and got down on the floor to go on with the work of smothering the fire. With what remained of the blackened blanket, he put out the last of it. The room was left in smoky blackness.

"I need a light," the doctor said.

"Right here!" called out Mrs. Lowry. She led the way with a candle as Martha followed with the water bucket. Just as the two came through the doorway, they were shoved aside by the boy who had been hiding in the store.

"Catch him!" Dr. Lowry yelled, but by then the boy was thudding around the side of the building.

Suddenly Jim snapped out of his daze. While the doctor poured water on the still-smoking floorboards, the boy bent to pick up his candle holder from the floor, righted the box, and set the candle on it after relighting it from the one Mrs. Lowry held. Now they could see the condition of the little room.

Mrs. Hood came in. "Oh, Jim," she said, looking at his hands. "You've burned your hands—and look at that shirt! You'll never be able to wear it again."

Jim picked up his shirt from the floor. It was the one his mother had made for him. He couldn't stop the tears that came to his eyes. His spare trousers—and even Jeremiah's—could never be worn again.

Mrs. Hood put her arm around his shoulders. "We're just thankful that you're all right, Jim—that you aren't burned anywhere else. We'll see that you have some new clothes. Those trousers were getting much too short anyway. Thank God we heard the yelling over here!"

The doctor picked up the charred blanket. The floor was blackened but not burned through. Where there was a little smoke, he poured the last of the water from the bucket Martha had brought. "I think we got it all out now," he said as he straightened up. "By the way, Jim, I nearly fell over your saddle just outside the door."

"Coy must have dropped it when he saw you," Jim said. "He and his buddies were hidin' in the store when I came in."

"That Colton will go to jail if he comes around here again," the doctor said. "I'll see to it personally."

Martha was looking at Jim. "I don't think he'll come back again, Daddy," she said.

A faint calling reached them from the house. "Oh my," said Mrs. Hood. "I'd better go back and tell Robert that everything is all right."

"We'll go, too," Dr. Lowry said. "I've got to get some ointment from my bag for Jim's burns."

Suddenly Jim remembered the paper in his pocket. He pulled it out and unfolded it. As he saw the first words of the letter—*Dere Jimboy*—he looked up with a broad smile on his soot-smudged face. "I think I just found a message from Pa," he said.

He bent over near the candle to let the light shine on the stained, wrinkled page. "Want to hear it?" he asked after quickly scanning it. The grin on his face told the Lowrys all was well.

He began to read aloud.

Dere Jimboy, I am sending this with J. J. to tell you my plans. I heerd of rich beaver sine north of here in the mts. I did not git as much money as we will be needin, so I am goin trappin for the winter to git sum more for us. I lernt a lot sins I left you. This life is ruff, & I had better lern more before I bring my only son out here.

So Jimboy pleez fergive me. I jest could not come back as things wuz. Pleez stay with the Hoods for the winter. They are good peeple & I no you will be a lot better off than if you wuz to come here now. I will send money for you so you can come. Likely in the spring. Wen you git it, come with the next carevan. J. Jones is bringin you the new saddle I got for you. I hope you like it.

I no you will understand Jimboy. Work hard & ern yur keep this winter. I no you will do rite like yur ma taut you to do.

Jim's voice broke for a moment, and he realized then that he had done the right thing in spite of himself. He was almost glad that word from his pa had been delayed this long. He'd learned a lot in the last couple of weeks.

Outside there was the sound of rain falling gently on the thirsty ground. Pedro would have grass to eat.

Jim looked up at Martha. Her eyes were shining.

"See, Jim? This is the way it's supposed to be."

Jim smiled. Suddenly all the gloom was gone. He knew now that he could choose for himself the way to go. No one, not even Coy, could make his decisions for him or make him do anything he didn't choose to do. He thought of Kit and Pedro out there on the trail, feeling the good rain. Kit had decided for himself, too, and he would live with whatever problems he had. For now, Jim was glad he was here.

His voice was steady as he finished reading the letter. "So, Jim-boy," he read aloud, "in the spring you can saddle up for Santa Fe, and you and me will go on together. Your loving Pa."

He looked up from the letter.

"Soon's I wipe the raindrops off my saddle, I'll be over to the house," he said to Mrs. Hood. "Never did finish my soup—I'm hungry, and I want to be ready for a good day's work tomorrow!"

DATE DUE

Wightwood Library
Wightwood School
56 Stony Creek Road
Branford, CT 06405
(203) 481-0363